She was alone in the windowless tower room

She'd been very careful not to make a sound. Then a tiny stir in the air made her turn around. The door was closing . . . slowly, quietly. As she started toward it, it slammed shut.

She clutched at the doorknob, but it turned loosely in her hand, useless. She pushed at the door. . but it was locked.

She banged her fists on the door and cried out, but something in the resonance of her voice told her the room was soundproof. She clenched her fists and fought her rising panic, then slowly began examining the crumbling walls for a hidden door. There was nothing.

Gradually she became aware of something else. The room smelled different. The stale odor of a moment ago was overlaid with another smell.

It was gas. . . .

THE RAVENS OF ROCKHURST

MARIAN MARTIN

Harlequin Books

TORONTO • NEW YORK • LONDON
AMSTERDAM • PARIS • SYDNEY • HAMBURG
STOCKHOLM • ATHENS • TOKYO • MILAN

Published July 1983
ISBN 0-373-32002-7

Printed in Canada

CHAPTER ONE

COURTNEY HUGHES STOOD BREATHLESSLY in the office of the Broberg Auction Gallery—"Seattle's Finest," the ads always said—waiting for her boss's decision. The hope and eagerness in her face gave her an elfin charm, erasing the grief and worry that had shadowed her features for the past year. Her short dark hair had a wayward mind of its own, but today it lay in well-behaved curls against her pale skin, as if it, too, were awaiting Rudi Broberg's answer.

Her sorrow over her father's death had transformed her from a carefree girl with a soft round face to a young woman of twenty-two whose face revealed a finely wrought beauty. But Courtney, never vain, had been too overwhelmed by her loss and the changes in her life to pay much attention to her appearance. She knew she was neat and clean, but beyond that, her notion of herself was hazy.

Mr. Broberg gave a deep sigh and shook his shaggy white head. He didn't relish sending Courtney on this assignment. It called for someone older, more experienced. He had known Courtney since she was a child, and he found it hard to believe that, even with her training, she was capable of handling this job. According to the correspondence with the widow Padgett, there was a large collection of art goods, china, glass, pottery and sculpture to be evaluated and a sale to be arranged. A big undertaking.

He gazed at Courtney's slight figure as she stood before him, her hands clasped together almost in an attitude of pleading. The surge of anger he felt whenever he thought of the mass of debts Robert Hughes had left this child when he died suffused his round face with red. How did a junior college art teacher obtain so much credit, he wondered, not for the first time. The debts that Robert left had come as a shock to Courtney, and Rudi Broberg had explained, as the lawyers had, that Courtney had no legal obligation to shoulder the burden of paying them off. But no one could dissuade her. It was her moral duty, she insisted. Now she wanted this assignment, her first real responsibility beyond clerking in the auction gallery, in order to earn more money toward repaying those debts.

Ach, she will never learn, this one, he thought. With a gesture of exasperation, he got up to come around the desk. She had even lost a young man through her stubbornness. What was his name— Kenny something—had left her rather than take on Robert's debts as a condition of marriage. *You see, Robert Hughes, what you have done,* he thought. But because Courtney had refused to recognize Robert's utter selfishness, he merely said aloud, "It is too much for you, this job. Better I send Albert. He has the experience."

Her dismay and disappointment showed in her face. "Mr. Broberg, I can do it, I know I can. And I'll never get the experience unless you give me an assignment."

"Ach, but such a big one. A month you'd be gone, maybe more."

"Within a few hours of Seattle. It wouldn't be as if I couldn't get home if I wanted to."

There was a long pause. With a sigh, he put a chunky but gentle hand under her chin, lifting her face and looking down into eyes grown large in her grief-lined face. "This is what you must do, then. The first thing goes wrong up there at this...this Rockhurst, you must come home."

It took a second for his meaning to sink in, then she burst out, "Oh, thank you. I'll do such a good job for you. You'll see." Impulsively she threw her arms around him and, standing on tiptoe, kissed his cheek. She jumped back, looking up quickly to see if he was angry at this unusual familiarity. But he was smiling, his cheeks ruddier than ever as if with pleasure.

They sat down to discuss the detail of the assignment, and after she left the office, Rudi Broberg sat gazing at the door. Courtney's spontaneous gesture of pleasure had been the first sign that her spirit was recovering since Robert's death and that young scamp's defection. She had been too quiet, too hard working, and he had worried helplessly about her. It was good to see a light in her eyes again. He hoped nothing would happen at Rockhurst to extinguish it. He hoped he was doing the right thing in letting her go up there, but he felt strangely unsure.

THREE DAYS LATER Courtney guided her old VW around still another hairpin curve high in the Cascade Mountains on her way to Rockhurst. She had been driving since ten that morning, leaving Seattle as soon as the gallery had opened. For the whole trip, her mind had been full of fears about her first assignment.

What would her reception at Rockhurst be like? She knew that at twenty-two, slim and fragile looking, she was not what Jacob Padgett's widow was expecting. Would Mrs. Padgett agree to put her entire collection, worth a sizable fortune, into the hands of a young, inexperienced art appraiser? Mrs. Padgett knew Courtney was a woman, but Rudi had left out the other details.

She had wanted this assignment very much. For if old Jacob Padgett really had stuffed his house with art treasures, as his widow's letters had promised, this job was just what she'd been hoping for. She would make a complete inventory and appraisal and arrange a wonderfully successful sale. And after that, Mr. Broberg would have to take her seriously as an art dealer—or at least as a respected apprentice. That would be the means, she thought, of working out her problem—her father's problem, really.

She stopped at Harrington's General Store and Post Office, then for the next five or six miles she saw no living soul. Not that there wasn't life on Mt. Kulshan. At one point she barely missed hitting a deer that materialized from the brush and stood for a moment in the center of the road. Chipmunks darted anxiously across the road, and a large squirrel stared from a mossy rock. She knew there were other animals, too, sleeping through the heat of the day behind the screen of bearberry and salal: raccoons and possums and owls, awaiting their time to prowl the silent woods.

The hot wind swirled the red dust of disintegrating fir and pine needles through the window, leaving powder on her hands and arms and turning her hair a rusty brown. Finally, with relief, she saw the carved wooden sign arching over the turnoff: ROCKHURST. And under it in smaller letters: J. PADGETT. She swung the VW onto the side road, which had narrowed down now to little more than a tunnel through the trees, and began the climb up the twisting grade.

As she drove, she caught glimpses of the house through a wall of greenery. Rockhurst was built in the nineties, when people wanted room to move and details to delight the eye. Shaped chimneys rose above carved eaves; fretted railings trimmed myriad balconies. A turret with a domed roof shone with a diadem of filigreed brass. It was a house for telling fairy tales, Courtney thought. Or for living them. As she stared, three ravens bolted into the air and circled the tower in great soaring arcs, as if draping it in doleful black ribbons.

But this wasn't what she'd had in mind for her first assignment, she thought, looking up at this strange sad house. She'd imagined some place in town, so she could go home every night to her two rooms on the third floor, with her cat Maynard clawing the slip covers, and the neighbor's stereo throbbing beyond the wall. Not this huge house brooding in the unearthly quiet.

Courtney pulled the VW behind an old maroon station wagon in the drive. There was something comforting about the prosaic Chevy wagon, she thought, a tie to the outside world. Shutting off the car's engine, she sat for a moment, trying to pull herself together and gather her thoughts. It was so important that she make the right impression from the very start. She must make the people here want to give her the commission. A good job here would mean other chances and further commissions to help pay her father's bills. All she needed was the chance.

And all she had to do was go against all her instincts to run from what was new and strange and therefore dangerous—all her tendencies to tiptoe cautiously past anything unfamiliar. But she had long ago learned that being afraid didn't necessarily stop a person from going ahead and doing what had to be done.

She got out of the car, trying to brush some of the red dust from her suit. The tailored navy blue outfit was supposed to make her look unafraid, efficient and businesslike. Instead, she was afraid it made her look all the younger and more vulnerable. A quick breeze awakened a long branch of the Paul's scarlet rose that swayed, parched and dull, from the pillar of the porte cochere. The branch groped through the air, searching for her hair and shoulder. She pushed it aside, pricking her finger on a thorn, and marched up the broad wooden steps, feeling like an innocent person unfairly condemned.

She stood for a long time after she rang the bell, dutifully noticing the stained-glass margin lights of the door, the brass fittings and the bell itself—all collectible Victoriana now. At last the door opened and a woman stood squarely in the doorway, her dough-face stony as Courtney identified herself. The woman's olive green cotton dress was clean and starched, but too large, as if she'd lost weight or hadn't bothered to find her correct size.

Finally she stepped aside and said, "In here," directing Courtney to a sitting room just off the entrance. As Courtney passed through the central hall, she noted the maroon-and-rose carpets, heavy carved doors on three walls, an impressive sweeping staircase.

She was surprised to see that the woman had followed her into the sitting room and now stood looking at her. Trying to hide her discomfort, Courtney asked if Mrs. Padgett had been told she was there.

"Oh, she knows you're here. There aren't so many cars that pull into the place that she'd miss one. Besides, she's been waiting for you since noon." A disdainful smile twisted her thin lips. "Can't wait to turn all this into nice hard cash."

Courtney looked at the two Sheraton china cabinets standing against the wall. They were nearly empty, and the little bric-a-brac they held was a long way from art. There were a couple of shepherdesses in inferior cloudy ceramic and a covey of gaudy birds. If this was what Jacob Padgett had spent years collecting, she had come a long way for nothing. Only her determination to show Mr. Broberg that she could do this job—if there was a job to do—kept her from turning on her heels that moment. Her dismay showed in her face.

"This ain't the stuff." The woman's laugh was short and harsh. "It's out there." She jerked her head toward the center of the house. "And upstairs, and in the shed, and God knows where else."

Courtney longed to ask her what the "stuff" was

like, how much of it there was, whether it was any good. But she didn't know who the woman was. Housekeeper? Companion? Neighbor? She hadn't introduced herself, and Courtney didn't know how to ask her. Besides, it wouldn't do to discuss the client's business with a third party, no matter who the person was.

Courtney glanced at the woman and away again, intimidated by her severity. She had steel-gray hair pulled into a bun, and full jowls and a bulbous nose free of makeup. No vanity here, Courtney thought. Nothing as soft as vanity. Instead there was something very strong. Something, perhaps, that bound her to a purpose. Wistfully, Courtney hoped it was a friendly purpose. She smothered her impatience as well as she could, but she wished Mrs. Padgett would hurry.

As if conjured up by her thoughts, there was a sound of voices outside the door—a man's and a woman's—punctuated by the shattering of glass. The woman beside Courtney jumped and muttered, "Damn fool." She pulled the door partly open, but a small gray-haired woman—surely Mrs. Padgett, Courtney thought—clung to the door with one hand and the doorjamb with the other, bracing herself and blocking the doorway.

"Now what was that all about?" the severe-looking woman demanded.

The small woman shook her head as if coming out of a bad dream. She looked around, blinking. "Nothing. No one. It doesn't matter."

"Doesn't matter? Listen, you going to let them do you that way?"

"No one's done anything." She pulled herself up with fragile dignity. "But there's been an accident. One of the Tiffany vases has been knocked over. Would you see to getting it cleaned up, please?"

"Accident! Ha!"

"Jenny."

"I'm going. As fast as I can." She clumped out of the room.

The small woman turned to Courtney, one slender blue-veined hand extended. "I'm Sarah Padgett. And you're the young lady from Broberg Gallery, of course. Courtney Hughes, isn't it? Welcome to Rockhurst, Courtney."

Mrs. Padgett had obviously taken great care with her appearance. So much care that Courtney wondered if she was as nervous about this meeting as Courtney herself. But that couldn't be, she thought. Why would Mrs. Padgett be nervous? Unless the collection wasn't as good as she had claimed, Courtney thought with a sinking heart.

She smiled through her momentary dismay and concentrated on saying the correct things. But as she got her first good look at the mistress of Rockhurst, she felt herself slipping into a swampy confusion. Time seemed to be spinning backward—or sideways. Jacob Padgett, she and Rudi had gathered from Sarah's letters, had been nearly ninety, apparently much older than his wife, who was probably in her late sixties. But Courtney's confusion arose not from Sarah Padgett's age, but from her dress. She was a period piece, set down into the wrong time slot.

The house was turn-of-the-century, but Mrs. Padgett's short teal-blue crepe dress was from a different

era. It had padded shoulders and a ruffled peplum.
An artificial gardenia was pinned to her lapel. Her
teal shoes were high-heeled, with crossed ankle
straps. Shiny, fat curls were piled on top of her head.
Except for the fact that her hair was silver gray instead of gold, she looked like a pin-up girl from a
World War II movie. Courtney was struck by the
thought that she'd stepped into a place whose in-
habitants chose a year he or she liked and stayed
there, regardless of whether it was a different year
from everyone else's.

She tried to shake the image and concentrate on
reality, but it wasn't easy as she and Sarah observed
the small ritual civilities. As they talked, Courtney
studied the sculptured curls, the pale blue eye
shadow, the faintly rouged cheeks.

"You know it will take you quite some time to
study all of Jacob's lovely things," Mrs. Padgett was
saying. "You'll stay with us of course, and be...."
She stopped and dropped her gaze. "I was going to
say one of the family." A shadow flickered across
her face. "Perhaps a guest, a very special guest,
would be better." Impulsively, she reached across
and put her tiny hand on Courtney's. "I'll be so glad
to have someone here to talk to."

Courtney's heart went out to her. She remembered
what it was like to lose someone dear and close. She
knew the aching emptiness of the room where her
father would never again sit and talk to her. So this
was why Mrs. Padgett had taken pains to look her
best, Courtney thought. She was isolated here on Mt.
Kulshan, perhaps without any other woman except
the sour-faced housekeeper. But Mrs. Padgett

wouldn't put her feelings into words, or play for sympathy. Courtney thought she was very brave and that her own worries about making a good impression had been wasted. Poor little Mrs. Padgett would have accepted her, no matter what.

The housekeeper came back with a tea tray, and Mrs. Padgett introduced her, saying, "Jenny's been with me for years, haven't you, Jenny?"

"Since the beginning," Jenny said. "Since before you *was* Mrs. Jacob Padgett."

"Yes, of course." She patted Jenny's arm and got no response. "And Jenny *will* do everything she can to help you." The eyes of the two older women met and held for a long second. Courtney couldn't tell who looked away first—gentle Sarah, who was anxious for everything to go right, or Jenny, who no doubt had her own ideas about how things should be.

"And you needn't worry about. . . the Boys or anyone else," Mrs. Padgett said as she turned her attention to pouring the tea. "My grandson, Aaron, or my grandnephew, Daniel. No matter what they say, pay them no mind." She passed Courtney a cup of tea and sat back, very straight and proper. Like a prim, gray-haired doll, Courtney thought. "Everything in the house is mine." She smiled at the tiny whirlpool her spoon made in her cup. "Whatever they say, it's all mine."

As Courtney listened, her professional side noted the cup and saucer, made of heavy cheap pottery. It was what her father used to call bank-night china, because it was given away at movie houses on bank night during the Depression. Could a household where people ate from bank-night china really hold a fortune in art?

"The only thing I'm concerned with is the collection," Courtney assured her. She wasn't going to be stampeded by this mite of a woman, with her piled-up curls and her wistful air, into getting involved in family matters. Her only aim was to get all the information she could on the size and scope of Jacob Padgett's collection.

Sarah Padgett's letters had said that Jacob had collected a good deal of Chinese jade and several very good icons. One of Courtney's specialities was Chinese art; religious icons another. This was the main reason Mr. Broberg had even considered her for this job. The weight of her coming decision depressed her. If she decided Jacob's collection wasn't worthwhile, she could leave with no blame attached... unless six months from now some rival gallery had a tremendous success with the "Padgett Sale." If she misjudged, it would be the end of her hopes in the art field.

And if she decided to stay—if she committed herself to an inventory and sale—there would be no turning back. When her father died, his old friend Rudi Broberg had hired Courtney to work full time. He never expressed regret at hiring her, but after more than a year, she hadn't broken through his unconscious Old World chauvinism that wouldn't allow her to be more than a floor clerk, a dustman and, occasionally, a secretary. Her years with him before her father's death, as a part-time trainee while she was at art school, seemed to have made no impression on him. Rudi Broberg was more than a boss, he was a dear friend—but a determinedly stubborn one.

Sarah—she insisted everyone call her that—was chattering on, asking Courtney why such an attractive young girl would agree to come to the mountains for such a long time, "away from the city and all your young men."

Courtney hesitated, considering how to tell Sarah that her stock of young men had narrowed down to one, and then last year, the one had blown away, leaving only a note from the airport and one postcard from New York. Courtney could understand why Ken hadn't been willing to wait to start their life together until after she finished paying off her father's debts. It was slow going on her salary, and there were a lot of bills. Although, as the months had passed, she had learned to accept his decision, it continued to be nearly as painful for her to think about as when she had first read his words in the note. It was all too complicated to explain to Sarah, however, and she was sure Sarah wasn't interested in her personal life. So she said, "It's only for a month, you know."

"A month, yes. And you think that'll be gone before you can blink your eyes, don't you?" Sarah sighed and carefully put her cup down on the table. "My dear, a world can stop in a month. Doors close, chances vanish." Her dry cheeks became ever paler, leaving the touch of rouge to stand out in startling contrast. "Everything can change in a month."

Courtney assumed Sarah was thinking of her own dark plunge into widowhood and murmured an agreement. But for her, there was little to lose. Even after her father's sudden death and Ken's defection—which were exceptions to the rule, she thought—the word "change" still meant "improve." She wished a month *would* change everything. She wanted her whole life to be different, shaken up and turned around. But on that sunny afternoon, she didn't know all the meanings of change, or how true the old lady's words were.

"You'll not...you'll not be bringing anyone up here, will you?" Sarah asked after a moment.

"Bringing...? Oh, you mean some man." Courtney smiled. "There isn't any young man on the horizon at the moment."

"There isn't? My goodness, the young men today must be blind. Why, when I was your age...." Sarah's thin hand fluttered in the air. "Perhaps you are too...particular."

"Perhaps," Courtney said, smiling, and added to herself, *and getting choosier all the time.* Not that she'd have men flocking around, as Sarah implied. She was really a very ordinary girl, with plain looks and no style or glamour. Perhaps that was what she'd like to change, she thought.

"I'm afraid you'll not find many...diversions here," Sarah said, and warned Courtney against losing her heart to "the Boys."

Conjuring up a vision of the Boys as a middle-aged Tweedledee and Tweedledum, Courtney assured her there was no chance her heart would be lost, not adding that it was too bruised and battered to stray far.

"Of course, we do have our moments here," Sarah went on. "Especially when Winston comes to call. Winston Coe—he has a summer place a mile or so up the road." Her eyes drifted to the past. "He used to

talk to Jacob about Jacob's things. Knows everything about art, you know.'' She giggled and added,
''Then he'd talk to me about what summer visitor
was chasing which local girl.'' Her face wrinkled with
amusement.

Poor thing, Courtney thought. She had little
enough to amuse her. But Courtney felt no need of a
gossipy art lover to lighten her off-hours. And
charming men, like Ken and her father, had left her
with only a broken romance and a pile of debts.
From now on, she would concentrate on her work
and let the charmers go charm someone else.

After they had talked for nearly an hour, Sarah
proposed turning Courtney over to Jenny for a tour
of the house and an introduction to part of the collection, while she herself rested. Although Courtney
was slender and of less than average height, she felt
big standing next to Sarah. She did some rapid cal-
culations and decided Sarah must have been a young
woman when World War II broke out. Had her life
stopped then? Was she trying to preserve that time
like dried rose petals?

Sarah called, in a high piping voice, and Jenny instantly appeared in the doorway. Courtney wondered
if she had anticipated Sarah's routine of resting each
afternoon, or if she had been standing just outside
the door listening.

Courtney followed Jenny up the sweeping stair-
way, which was lit by panels of stained-glass roses
and lilies. Each baluster of the hand-carved railing
was wreathed in acanthus leaves and ivy. On the
newel post at the foot, carved faces of the four winds
blew eternally into the hall. Jenny looked wryly

amused as Courtney exclaimed over the wealth of detail and the charm of the design. Jenny assured her dryly that she'd get used to "all them gewgaws" and not see them after a while. She certainly couldn't let that happen, she thought with amusement. Gewgaws, in a manner of speaking, were her business.

The staircase impressed her by its size and ornamentation, and perhaps because it was the first feature of the house that she was able to examine closely. But by the time she was settled in her room, her eyes had begun to glaze over. She was fatigued by the onslaught of rich design, by beauty too lavishly used, by jewellike details jammed together. The house, she thought, was everything Diamond Jim Brady or Molly Brown could have wanted.

She hung up her yellow linen sundress and a long gray skirt in the huge, ornately carved walnut armoire, but left everything else as it was. Her working clothes—slacks and shirts—her price guides, her needlepoint, could all wait until she knew whether or not she would stay. So far, the beauties of the house were permanent fixtures, not things she could wrap up and ship back to the auction gallery. She didn't yet know what else Rockhurst held, but she hoped it would be more portable than the gilt chandelier and marble mantelpiece she found in her bedroom.

Puzzling her way through a labyrinth of corridors, she went down the stairs to the library to meet Jenny and begin her tour of inspection. She found the room empty, but with one glance around, her hopes for the collection surged. High narrow bookcases were spaced around the room like pilasters. Near the fireplace, the pattern was broken where two bookcases had been replaced with glass-fronted cabinets. Behind locked doors one cabinet held china figurines; the other held Jacob Padgett's jade.

Courtney's practiced eye skimmed over the elaborate overmantel with its burden of porcelain—could those be real Staffordshire dogs?—and the brace of pistols flanking the fireplace; she made a mental note to send for a catalog on firearms. A desk, its top obscured by several piles of papers, sat in front of the fireplace. Like the rest of the house, the desk was heavily ornamented, and oversized. But the jade...! A surge of excitement caught her.

With real pleasure, Courtney turned to examine the double-locked jade cabinet. There were several Buddhas, an old dignified fisherman, some bowls and the goddess Kuan Yin. There were pieces ranging in color from the green of dark ivy of the palest green found at the heart of a rose; there was pink, white and lavender jade. None of the pieces looked really ancient to Courtney; there was nothing from before the Ch'ing dynasty. But every piece was beautifully executed, and she was sure it was all prerevolution. Kneeling in front of the cabinet, she tried to see around to the back of a small lavender jade Buddha, of gemstone quality, who watched benignly from the lowest shelf. She was so engrossed she didn't realize anyone else was in the room until she saw the heavy boots and work pants of a man standing beside her.

Startled, she turned to see two men and knew they had to be Aaron, the grandson, and Daniel, the grandnephew. Both men stood rooted, and for a moment Courtney wondered if she could have been mistaken, that these were the Boys after all; for they were younger than she had expected. Both men wore shirts buttoned at the wrists and neck, which she knew was a woodsman's protection against ticks and spiders and sharp twigs. She caught her breath as she turned her gaze to the taller man. She had never seen such an arresting face—darkly handsome and compelling, with a fine nose and chin—a face all made up of angles and deeply etched lines. She wondered if the lines had been drawn by weather or by suffering.

The smaller blond man stepped forward. "Hi, I'm Daniel Padgett," he said. He was everything the other man was not: open, friendly, welcoming. "I surely do hope there's something we can do for you, pretty lady." His smile seemed to light up the dim room.

"I'm Courtney Hughes. I—"

"Well, Courtney Hughes, welcome to Rockhurst," Daniel said. "And this fountain of small talk is my cousin, Aaron Padgett. Say hello to the nice lady, Aaron."

Aaron, the dark one, seemed to be the older of the two, perhaps in his early thirties. Above fierce black eyes set broodingly deep, his eyebrows joined in a smudged bar of disapproval. Hostility was plain in his face, as if Courtney were somehow a threat to him.

But that was impossible, she thought. She could never be a danger to the man who was towering over her, looking like a Rodin statue, as hard and burnished as bronze. Thinking she would never even want to be a threat to him, she found to her dismay that her hands were shaking. She forced herself to look away to the blond cousin, who suddenly grinned engagingly.

"Well, you can't be the Courtney Hughes who's come to put a price on all our ornaments and baubles," he said. "We were expecting a plump middle-aged man with a pince-nez on a black ribbon and a shiny leather briefcase."

She laughed, tempted to tell him that she had expected the same. "I have the briefcase," she offered.

"Then you must be the right Courtney Hughes."

"Surely Mr. Broberg—Rudi Broberg, my boss—in his letters he told Mrs. Padgett that I was...that I am...." She spluttered to a halt.

"That you're so pretty and not plump or middle-aged?" He looked at her appreciatively, and she did her best to hide her annoyance. "Well, pretty lady, your boss probably did tell Sarah. But she doesn't confide in us much these days."

His words reminded Courtney that he and his dark-haired cousin were not responsible for the collection. She would have no trouble following Sarah's advice to "pay them no mind." She looked at Daniel coolly. He wore carefully cut slacks and a shirt that was just a hair too tight across his muscular chest and shoulders. Vain, she thought. But at least he looked friendly, unlike his cousin, Aaron.

The contrast between the two men went beyond their faces and coloring. Aaron's green-and-black plaid cotton shirt was tucked into whipcord work pants that were frayed at the pockets. And instead of a welcoming smile, he looked at her as if she were bringing a suitcase full of tussock moths to let loose in his stand of timber

No one had ever looked at her like that before. She supposed there had been people who hadn't liked her, but no one had ever shown it so clearly. She was upset by his attitude. Well, who wouldn't have been, she told herself. But there was more to it than that. She should have been able to shrug it off, to say, so what? But she was disturbed by his antagonism, partly because she had done nothing that she knew of to deserve it, and partly, she had to admit, because she wanted him to like her. She wanted that dark Gypsy face to smile at her, wanted to hear the deep voice say, "Hello, Courtney," with warmth in it. She shook herself free of foolish daydreams as he said instead, "You're the art appraiser."

Her natural spunkiness reasserted itself, and she refused to be cowed by Aaron's superior attitude. But she resisted the impulse to say, "Yes, I know." She merely looked back at him.

Daniel rushed into the charged silence. "I hope you'll do everything you can to help Sarah."

"So you can get your share?" Aaron's voice was a growl.

That explained a lot, Courtney thought. It wasn't just her he disliked, it was everybody. Or perhaps it was just the situation, the sale of Jacob's art collection, that Aaron opposed.

Daniel laughed. "I have a claim to a share of Sarah's riches. The same as you do." He gave Aaron a good-natured slap on the shoulder.

But Aaron wasn't in the mood for playfulness—Courtney wondered if he ever was—and he turned his attention to the papers on the desk. Courtney went back to Daniel's comment about helping Sarah.

"I haven't decided yet whether I'll take the job of arranging a sale." She explained that she would need to know more about the collection and what was to be sold.

"Everything, as far as I know," Daniel said.

"Right down to the linoleum on the kitchen floor," Aaron put in from the desk. "Every stick of furniture on the place and the gold fillings in Sarah's teeth, if that's what you want and you've got the cash."

What a coldhearted cynic, she thought. Did he really think everyone was after nothing but money? She told herself again that it didn't matter what he thought. But she knew it did. It was disturbing and confusing, but she cared that this bronze giant didn't like her, and she cared that he was hardhearted and cold. Would his heart, like bronze, warm to the touch of a loving hand? Shocked at her errant thoughts, she turned sternly back to business and explained that she didn't have money and didn't buy directly.

"Too bad. You just lost Daniel's interest."

Courtney ignored him pointedly and went on. "I need to know if Miss Sarah will really go through with the sale once it's set up." She shrugged. "She seemed reluctant."

They both blinked at her and Daniel grinned. Even Aaron's face lost its grim set.

"Sarah? Are you sure you're talking about our Sarah?" Daniel asked. Then he added seriously, "Yes, she'll go through with the sale. She's very anxious to sell out, really. The inheritance tax took a big bite, and she's truly strapped for money."

"And there won't be any trouble, any last-minute interference from any other source?"

Daniel looked puzzled and Aaron said, "She means from us." Two steps across the hushed room brought him close to her. She caught her breath as she looked up into a face like a mountain storm. Strength radiated from him, and without ever touching her, he forced her helplessly back against the fireplace.

His voice was a low rumble. "Run back to Seattle, little girl, or San Francisco, or wherever you're from. You don't belong here."

She stared at him, frightened and angry and too astonished to speak.

"Do you hear? Get away. Quick."

"Now, don't intimidate the poor little thing," Daniel said. "All she wants to know is whether we're going to stop her from arranging a nice sale for Sarah." He spread his hands, palms up.

"We're as anxious to have Jacob's estate liquidated as Sarah is, Miss Hughes," Aaron said. "My advice to you is to leave; let someone else do this job. But if you're determined to stay, we won't stop you. You'll find us completely cooperative.'

Before she could sort out her feelings or find the words to strike back at this arrogant, superior oaf, he gathered up a sheaf of papers from the desk and left the room. Daniel said he'd be seeing her and, with a wink, followed Aaron out.

The Padgett cousins might have been anxious to have the estate turned into cash, but Courtney had no illusions about how cooperative they'd be. It was another item to add to her list of questions about this job. Would she be able to do it without their help?

And what was it that Daniel had said about having a claim to a share? Sarah had said, "It's all mine." What were they up to, these cousins who looked so different, but might be more alike than they appeared?

She was no further along in coming to a decision about taking the assignment...which was funny when she remembered how much she'd wanted it. If only there was something that would tip the scales one way or the other. She supposed that was wishful thinking. Decisions were only decisions if they were so nearly balanced that it was hard to tell which course was right and which wrong.

CHAPTER TWO

Before Courtney could make a thorough examination of the jade in Jacob Padgett's cabinet, she was interrupted once more, this time by an older, somehow defeated-looking man.

"I'm Floyd," he said by way of greeting. "Handyman and general flunky around here."

He was no more cordial than Jenny or Aaron had been. Like the Padgett cousins, his denim shirt was buttoned at the neck and wrists. He seemed to be all muscle, but Courtney wondered if the slackness of his face meant that there was no clear thought process behind the muscle.

"You want something done, you might's well ask me. You ask anyone else, they'll just make me do it anyhow."

His faded blue eyes were slits in the weathered face as he concentrated on what he wanted to say. Somehow, his defensive churlishness made him seem vulnerable to hurts and slights, and she felt sorry for him. She willed her face to do its best to look friendly, and apparently it satisfied him. He relaxed visibly.

"You the art buyer?" He stared at her. "You got to look at everything the old man had, right?" Bushy gray eyebrows shaded his eyes as he looked at her slyly. "But you got to find it first "

"I wish you'd help me if you can."

"I could tell you where everything in the whole house is, if I had a mind to."

She waited but he didn't go on until she reminded him it would be for Mrs. Padgett's good. Then he laughed and said, "Everything around here's for Mrs. Padgett's good, ain't it?" He paused, squinting at her. Then, as if coming to a decision, he went on. "Some of it's in the parlor and in the library here." The sly look returned. "And there's something else. Or was, if one of them thievin' boys ain't sold it by now."

"You got no right—" Jenny's voice cut through the air like a knife "—no right at all, Floyd Taylor, to talk like that. The old man's dead, and you ain't got the freedom to talk any old way you want no more." Jenny turned toward Courtney, starch stiff. "The old man encouraged him to think he was special." Jenny turned away austerely. "Miss Hughes ain't interested in your gossip, Floyd."

She was so right, Courtney thought. Only if the gossip affected the collection, or her judgment of it, was she interested. But Jacob's collection was in their bloodstreams, coloring their views, distorting their reactions. It was apparent that in this house she was not alone in feeling that the collection was all that mattered.

"There wasn't nothing he didn't collect," Jenny told her. "Anything he got his hands on, he kept. That's a kind of collecting, ain't it?"

Courtney nodded unhappily. Compulsive acquisition was a kind of collecting that art dealers were all too familiar with. It would make her decision about staying much harder if the good pieces, assuming there were any besides the jade, were buried under a lot of junk.

Jenny said Jacob had even kept the toys he had as a boy. Back in the nineties, an uncle had sent curios home from the Orient, and that had started Jacob's art collection.

"People he'd write to, they'd offer good money, but he never sold. Just bought." Jenny wiped the top of the cabinet with her apron. He had written to dealers and collectors "and nuts like hisself" all over the world, Jenny explained, using money from the business, wages due the loggers—or Jenny; anything he could, to buy more.

"On top of that, he was mean," Floyd said. "Meanest man I ever knew." A look of baffled anger filled his face, a look that might once have held his face together before defeat drained it, Courtney thought. Floyd turned accusing eyes on Jenny. "He'd come back from the grave if he knew she was fixing to sell everything off."

Jenny's head snapped up from her polishing. "What's she supposed to do? Eat them old... " She stopped herself. "You just get on about your work, Floyd Taylor."

Floyd left the room, sensing that this time, Jenny meant it. She was all business as she fished a small ring of keys from under her apron and opened the jade cabinet. She watched as Courtney examined the individual pieces and quickly moved to lock the door as Courtney put the last piece back. "Well, what do you think?" she demanded suspiciously.

"There are some very nice jades there."

"Very nice? Ain't there nothing there that's so specially valuable, so...beyond anything you've ever seen...." She licked her lips. "Something Jacob might have considered his 'treasure'? Not sentimental treasure, but real cash-value treasure?"

She told Courtney that Jacob had come to believe, during the last year or two of his life, that he owned an item, or items, of tremendous value. Courtney explained that most of his possessions would have appreciated over the years. Much art from the past had been destroyed by nature or by successive wars. Some of it had been secreted away by misers, and museums had taken pieces out of circulation. Increasing rarity would have multiplied the value of Jacob's collection just by the passing of time.

But the conviction that grew on Jacob was different, Jenny insisted. Something had taken a jump, creating value out of nothing. Courtney agreed that that could and occasionally did happen. "But it wasn't these. They were quite costly when he bought them."

"The Boys think it was the jade. That's why I keep them double locked."

"You don't think they'd...."

"Steal one of them? Or all of them?" Her voice was low and sharp, with a bitter tone of disillusionment. "Maybe. One of them might, anyway."

Courtney stared at her. Then she thought, why shouldn't one of them be capable of stealing from Sarah? The blond one, Daniel, vain and flippant and probably spoiled. And the dark one, Aaron. Why did the mere thought of him make her feel so odd? Hollow and light-headed and confused. Was she afraid of him, of his size and his menacing hostility? That must be it, of course. She pulled her thoughts back to the present as Jenny herded her out the door, then stopped, peering through the gloom of the big main hall.

Dropping her voice to a whisper, Jenny pressed close until Courtney could feel her warm breath on her cheek. "It just don't pay to take chances."

Courtney pulled away and said briskly that it was time she saw the rest of the house. With a shrug, Jenny obliged by showing her into the front parlor. Courtney was struck again by the similarity between a collector and a miser. The only difference was that the medium of exchange was not money. The vase, the stamp or the picture was the only coin he recognized, and these he gathered and admired, counted and hoarded as any miser would.

On a table just inside the door, porcelain figures and glass bowls and vases crowded together, all covered by a layer of dust. On the lower shelf a group of jasperware pieces—blue-and-white boxes, pots and bowls—were jammed around a copy of the dumpy Portland vase whose white classical Greeks were gray and grimy.

When Jenny said she'd long ago given up trying to dust the art goods, Courtney groaned inwardly at the thought of all the grime she'd have to work through to evaluate them.

Jenny said an inventory had been made for the court, to settle the estate, but it wouldn't do Courtney much good. Sarah hadn't been up to it, so Jenny and Mr. Hamill, the family lawyer, had done the best they could. Courtney smiled as she pictured the lawver's eyes glazing at the sight of all this china, some of it looking for all the world like Woolworth's best.

After half an hour of examining a small fortune in porcelain, some of it of museum quality, Courtney couldn't believe Jacob had accumulated so much by correspondence. Surely he had traveled to get certain pieces.

"Not the last few years, he didn't," Jenny said. "Used to go to Seattle, sometimes to San Francisco, years back, but not lately."

"Why did he stop his trips? His age?"

"Wasn't his age. Reason he didn't go was no one would go with him anymore, and he was... funny-like about being in the city alone. Of course, Sarah...." Jenny seemed to catch herself. "She didn't go," she finished flatly. "If one of them boys went, they'd just fight with him about spending the money. Can't blame them none."

Following Jenny across the central hall back to the stairs, Courtney tried to find a way to continue the conversation. She wanted to reach the housekeeper; Jenny could be very helpful to her in her work. But more than that, she wanted Jenny to like her. There was something about the hard-bitten, grumpy old woman that appealed to Courtney. From the time Courtney was little and her father had pushed her forward at faculty teas, whispering fiercely in her ear, "Just speak nicely. And smile, can't you? Make them like you," she had thought herself doomed to failure at making people like her.

She had learned to "speak nicely," but she had never learned to smile when she didn't mean it. And she had never learned how to make people like her. It always seemed to her that her friends liked her for some mysterious reason of their own, and in spite of any efforts she may have made.

Although conscious that she had nothing of interest to offer this angry, competent woman, she tried to start a friendly conversation anyway. As they climbed the great curving staircase, she tried the weather.

"Too hot and dry," Jenny snapped. "Fire hazard warning's been up a month or more."

Jenny stumped up the second flight as if she were crossing a level floor while Courtney commented on the wildlife she had seen on the drive up the mountain.

"Suppose you're *thrilled* with it." Jenny gave the word a working-over.

"Well...." Courtney had to catch her breath on the third flight. "It was interesting to see deer and squirrels and all."

"All right in its place, I guess," Jenny said, adding that a squirrel or a raccoon in the attic could be very annoying. There was a whole family of rabbits camped just outside the shed, she said, and if she was a good enough shot, she'd scatter them quick enough. They were eating the kitchen garden faster than Jenny could pick it. Aaron had put up a chicken-wire fence, "And that just gave them a good laugh. He won't set traps, and he says he's got no time to sit with a gun and wait for them to show up. Wouldn't take no more'n one daybreak, but he won't do nothin' he don't want to do. Specially if he thinks someone wants him to do it." She clumped down the narrow, dark third-floor hallway as Courtney hurried to keep up with her. "Just plain ornery is what he is. Always was, always will be."

Aaron sounded like a thoroughly difficult man to get along with, Courtney thought. But then, Jenny probably wouldn't make much effort to ask him nicely when she wanted his help.

At last Jenny stopped at a door and fumbled with her key ring. She opened the door and stepped aside, gesturing Courtney into a small room lit only by a north window. Fir branches filtered the light still more. Jenny struck a kitchen match and lit a kerosene lamp, explaining that Jacob had stopped the electrical wiring at the second floor. "Always claimed he ran out of money," she sniffed. "Everybody knows what happened was he found some new pot or something he wanted and used the money for that instead."

She unlocked a tall wooden cabinet built against one wall. The double doors opened to reveal a velvet-lined interior. On the sapphire-colored shelves stood five small icons, painted on wood cracked and darkened with age. A manger scene, with stiff primitive animals and a madonna of contrasting grace, was on the top shelf. The center shelf held a depiction of three saintly knights. The treatment was Byzantine, intricate in detail and lavished with gold. On the bottom was another madonna and a bishop, Saint Nicolas, dulled by the candle smoke of centuries.

"Maybe these are Jacob's treasure," Jenny said.

"Not if he was surprised at a sudden jump in value," Courtney said. She reached out to pick up one of the three saints. "These cost a fortune whenever he bought them." And as she returned the icon to its place, she knew she would stay on and arrange the sale. From the icons and the jade alone, she could realize a fine profit for Sarah. She felt too, that she should stay to protect Sarah from the Boys, perhaps even from Jenny and Floyd. Jenny might defend Sarah's right to sell the collection, but she didn't really seem anxious to see it go. Nor did Floyd. Perhaps they were afraid they'd be out of jobs and a home once Rockhurst was sold out. Maybe Aaron and Daniel weren't in favor of the sale, either, in spite of what they said. But Sarah Padgett was the heir, and only her wishes mattered.

"Made up your mind, haven't you?" Jenny said as she turned to lock up the cabinet. "If it was me and I didn't have no stake in what happened, there wouldn't be nothing could keep me here." Her eyes narrowed. "I got too many years invested to leave now before I get some of what's due me. But you... well, I just hope you know what you're doing."

More calmly than she felt, Courtney assured her there was nothing to worry about and said she'd need to see the rest of the collection, but needn't keep Jenny from her work. Still looking doubtful, Jenny returned to her duties, leaving Courtney on her own.

On the second-floor landing, Courtney noticed that the dimness was eased by the skylight overhead, but that vast shadowy feeling of the great staircase still enveloped her. She stood motionless for a moment, gazing down into the wide gray expanse of the central hall, when something—a presence, a sound— made her look up.

From the corner of her eye, registering quicker than she could think, she caught a movement. Or an impression of movement. Fear fluttered up like a swarm of bats and she pushed it away. It was a shadow from the firs, she told herself sternly, branches stretching to peer into the window. Or it might have been an animal; no one had mentioned a dog or a cat, but there was probably one around. It might have been her too-active imagination again. It was ridiculous even to feel these deep subliminal fears, these thumps of terror, she told herself. After all, she was in a civilized house, full of civilized human beings. All she had to do was call, and half a dozen people would be at her side in seconds.

She forced herself to take slow deep breaths until she had her emotions under control again. With a sheepish shake of her head, she turned toward her own room, half-resolved to change her mind about Rockhurst. She could throw her things together, say goodbye to Sarah Padgett and be back in Seattle before midnight.

Again a slight sound stopped her. In spite of thick walls and muffling carpets, the tiny noise was clearly audible in the utter silence of the house. But it was not an animal sound. It was more like a breathless hiccup, almost a sob. She followed the sound until she came to the room it was coming from. Courtney felt sure it was Sarah. The thin voice, with its quaver of age, would make just such a sobbing sound. She hesitated. Perhaps she should go away and tactfully pretend she had heard nothing.

Then she remembered Sarah's hand on hers, and Sarah's shining eyes as she said she was glad to have someone to talk to. Jenny would be little comfort with her hard bulbous face and her sharp voice. Nor would Daniel or Aaron. Perhaps Sarah would want to see her, she thought.

The door was slightly ajar, and when Courtney knocked, Sarah pulled it open right away. "Ah, Courtney, dear." She turned her head away and dabbed quickly at her eyes with a crumpled Kleenex. When she faced Courtney again, her chin was high. "Come in, please." She put a thin hand on Courtney's arm. "You heard a silly old woman crying and you came to help. I'm grateful to you." She sighed, making a gesture of invitation toward the room. "I'm afraid you caught me in a weak moment. It's very hard to be weak and all alone. There's no one to lean on and one just collapses." She stepped aside and Courtney entered a room much like her own, but larger and more ornate.

Curio shelves filled with ivory, and tables covered with porcelain figurines crowded against one another. One tall narrow window with a border of stained glass was swathed in folds of rose brocade. Rhododendron leaves peered over the sill, patterning the lace curtain in a dark dance. Carnation perfume spiced the air heavily.

On one wall was a display of fans, of lace, ivory and parchment, frozen at the instant of being flicked open. Courtney's first thought was that the lace should be in boxes, or under glass. Then she remembered why she was here and turned to Sarah.

"Is there anything I can do?" Courtney asked.

"Yes, there is, my dear." Sarah indicated a chair beside a tea table and motioned Courtney to sit opposite her. "You can reassure me, if it's possible, that I'm doing the right thing." She said that Jacob had loved each and every item, and because of that she hated to part with anything. "But you know, there isn't any money." She looked around the room at the ivory and the fans. "Every cent went into this."

"Collectors...something happens to them, and they forget there are other things, like bills to pay," Courtney said.

The old lady shook her head slowly, and a comb tucked into the sculptured gray curls glinted in the light. For the first time, Courtney realized that the comb and the button earrings in Sarah's perfect ears were studded with diamonds. Poverty-stricken and wearing diamonds? Well, why not, she thought. You can't eat diamonds, can you? Nor porcelain, nor jade.

"I've never had to make a decision like this before."

Courtney knew how she felt. She told Sarah that after she'd decided to sell her father's house to help meet some of the debts, things had begun to get easier. "It's the first step that's hardest."

"But how did you know it was the right thing to do?"

"I didn't," Courtney said. "You just have to hope." After everything was sold, she said, she found she didn't miss any of her old possessions. "What I mean to say is, the only thing you can take with you through the years is yourself."

"You sound too old and weary for a young girl."

"I feel weary sometimes," Courtney laughed. "Maybe it was the long drive up here that's doing it tonight."

Sarah studied her, ignoring her chatter. "Are you strong enough, Courtney? Is that self you take with you enough?"

"If it isn't, I'm in big trouble," she said. "Because there isn't anything else that lasts."

"You're wrong my dear. But I'll not try to convince you. When you're as old as I am, you'll know that two things are real and last. Two things last as long as time itself." Her voice had a sing-song quality, as if she were reciting, repeating well-learned lines to herself. She gazed through the window to a sky fading from white to blue as the day grew tired, a blank cloudless sky beyond the parched dull green fir needles. Into the silence her small voice dropped the words. "Two things. Love and hate."

After a moment, Sarah roused herself with a shake of her carefully cared-for head. "You have helped me a great deal, my dear. I think I can face what's coming, knowing that Jacob's art will be in good hands." She stood, and Courtney followed her to the door.

"Of course," Courtney cautioned, "one has to be careful...."

"Never fear, I am always careful." With a small private smile, she stood watching as Courtney hesitated at the landing, then went on down the stairs. When the girl was out of sight, Sarah's smile grew, and a small nod of satisfaction set the diamonds in her hair sparkling smugly.

As Courtney went down toward the central hall, she wished fervently there was something she could do that would be of real help to Sarah, something more tangible than mere reassurances.

She had never known her own mother, except in half-remembered, often-heard stories of birthday parties when her mother forgot to bake the cake, or zoo excursions where she got lost. The only feeling Courtney remembered having toward her mother was one of protectiveness. She remembered clearly taking her mother's hand at crosswalks because her mother sometimes forgot to look out for cars. Courtney wondered if Sarah's children ever felt that way about her. Then she remembered that Sarah had no children of her own. Only Aaron and Daniel.

She was glad she had decided to stay, in spite of Daniel with his too-easy charm and Aaron with his menacing anger; in spite of a staff that was full of malice and a mistress who was weak and confused and vain. Or perhaps it was because of all that she was glad she was staying.

Aaron couldn't frighten her away, and Jenny couldn't warn her away, not until she'd tried to find Jacob Padgett's "treasure." The rare find, the unexpected discovery was a lure that entranced all collectors and dealers. Against all odds, in spite of the probabilities, that was the enticement that Rockhurst held out, calling like a siren, drowning out all the apprehension and caution that Courtney might have felt.

Seeking a rest from the sensations and impressions that had poured in on her all day, Courtney headed for the front door and some fresh air. As soon as she stepped from the dim interior of the house onto the veranda, the heat slammed into her face like shocking news. She peeled off her suit jacket and draped it over the porch railing, then plunged into the full strength of the afternoon sun.

She followed the path around the house, circling the overgrown rhododendrons that spread across the path. Their leaves, shrouded in the reddish dust of powdered pine and fir needles, were dull and listless in the heat. Along the reddish-buff ground between the house and the outbuildings, the blinding light was broken only by the deep shade from an ancient mountain ash nearly as tall as the house's central tower. At first the only sounds she heard were a jay's call from somewhere deep in the woods, and the crack of something—a branch or a pine cone—falling to her right.

From the open door of a shed that stood wall to wall with the huge barn, a big dog, part German shepherd, part stranger, padded into the sunshine. Courtney stood still and let him come to her as she looked at the two buildings. Paint was peeling from the square sturdy shed, depositing flaky white chips, like dandruff on the red dust, along the base of the wall and on the worn doorstep. Once the dog had circled her and put his cold nose in her hand, they started together toward the open shed door.

It was the sound of voices that had drawn her—the Padgett cousins' voices—but as she drew closer, she realized they were angry voices, beating the air like blows from a powerful fist.

"Where did the money go? That's what I want to know."

"You know where it went." Aaron's voice was unmistakable. "If you hadn't encouraged the old man to spend every cent . . . ."

Courtney was just turning away to slip off before she was noticed, when Aaron saw her. "Interesting, isn't it? The loving family at work together."

Courtney's face flushed as if she had been caught purposely listening, and the injustice of that left her speechless. Aaron's taunting voice went on. "Perhaps there's something else you'd like to know. No need to hang about. Just come in and ask." He made a sweeping gesture as if inviting her into the small room, which had been converted to an office. Stiffly, she assured him his personal business was of no interest to her. She started to turn away, then stopped. There was something she wanted to know more about—this so-called treasure Jenny spoke of. She really didn't want to speak to Aaron, and she certainly didn't want him to think that anything he had to say was of the least importance to her. But the treasure, if there was one, had a bearing on the sale she would be arranging for Sarah. She owed it to her to find out whatever she could. She stepped out of the brilliant sunlight into the cool dim interior of the little office. Hesitantly she asked if they knew of anything that had taken a tremendous and surprising leap in value lately.

"You listen to gossip, don't you?" Aaron accused. Courtney backed away until the counter running along one wall stopped her. "You listen long enough," he said, "and you'll hear anything you want to hear."

"Lay off, Aaron," Daniel said.

"No. She wants to hear all about these things."

She couldn't defend herself, because it was true. She had been listening to the help's gossip. She looked up into his deep-set dark eyes and felt a shiver run through her body.

"You'll hear that Daniel's a leech and I'm a bastard, both of us living off the old man. The truth is, we've worked ourselves stupid for years to make this logging operation pay while he poured money into his vases and pots. You'll hear he hid a treasure somewhere. Truth is—"

"Now, that might be true, little one," Daniel told her.

"True, my foot." Aaron's voice was a growl.

"It could be." Daniel shrugged, and his smile came on full force. "Something in that pile of junk might be worth a fortune. Jacob said no one would ever guess where it is. He'd gloat about it, but he was surprised, too. And true or not, he believed it."

Here at last was something she could use. "Did he think it was something that had skyrocketed in value?"

"Exactly." Daniel grinned. "Intriguing?"

It was more than intriguing. "What do you think?" she asked him carefully. "Is there a treasure somewhere?" She could discount as idle gossip what Jenny had said. But what Daniel and Aaron thought was different. Daniel paused a moment before answering. She was afraid to breathe. So much depended on his answer.

"I think...it's unlikely."

Aaron snorted.

"Possible, but unlikely," Daniel added. "He knew so much about his goods that for him to be surprised by any part of it would be very odd."

She let her breath out. Daniel's answer was reasonable; it was unusual for an experienced collector to be caught by surprise. And yet. . . there was always that chance. And hadn't he said that Jacob himself believed in the sudden bonanza?

Aaron flatly disbelieved in the treasure. Or did he? The idea suddenly occurred to her that he "doth protest too much." Certainly he wanted her out of Rockhurst, and he wasn't going to let the possibility of the treasure's existence lure her into staying. But perhaps there was more to it than that.

Courtney let her mind play over the possibilities. If she could find something rare and wonderful and valuable, really valuable, amid the clutter of Jacob Padgett's acquisitions. . . . If she could recognize its worth when she saw it. . . . Her head spun with the possibilities. A smile and a nod from Mr. Broberg, maybe even a guttural, "Good work." Then more assignments, better commissions. Her father's debts paid at last, and the way open for her to begin living her own life.

Aaron interrupted her fantasy. "If you're counting on that, you're wasting your time," he warned. "It wouldn't be beyond Jacob to have planted the treasure rumor out of pure malice." As he turned toward her, his eyes narrowed, eyes so dark they were almost black, with the dim light of the office window reflected in them like sparks off steel. She caught her breath at the hardness—was it hatred?—she saw there. "He was mean, Jacob was, and sly as a fox. He. . . ." Aaron stopped himself. In the silence, she could hear the jay still calling, joined now by the demanding caws of a raven. The hot wind rustled through the firs. In a moment, Aaron went on. "He was a collector. What was his remained his." Although his voice was flat, she sensed the sorrow behind his words.

She had met collectors at the galleries, Courtney said; she knew what they could be like. "Collecting becomes an obsession, and nothing and no one else matters. They'd sell their wives and children for the one missing piece that would complete their collections."

Aaron seemed surprised and pleased that she understood. Even as she told herself she wasn't interested in his approval, she felt herself warming to his nod of agreement. He corrected her on one point, however. "The old man wouldn't have sold his wife and child. They belonged to him, too." The bitterness in his voice brought her back to reality and frightened her. They stood, staring into each other's eyes for a long moment. Then he said, "You shouldn't be here. You're not... you're not fitted for this job."

"Because I'm a woman? Your grandmother...."

"Sarah doesn't need you or want you here."

She clamped her mouth shut over the accusation that he was lying. But she thought she knew why he was doing it.

"You'll only fail and make it that much harder for all of us."

Fail at what? Arranging a sale, evaluating Jacob's collection? Or did Aaron think she'd fail at finding Jacob's treasure? Who did he think he was, deciding for others what they should do? Clearly, he had been running Rockhurst, directing the logging, ruling everyone, except perhaps Jacob, for a long time. But

Sarah wanted her to stay, she knew that. She lifted her chin to hide the anger that made her tremble. What a confusing man he was, oppressed one moment and oppressor the next.

Before she could find adequate words to answer him, Daniel took her arm and turned her to the door, saying it was time he showed her around the place. "C'mon, Toby." The big dog, dozing fitfully under the counter, laboriously got up and came to Daniel's side. "You mustn't mind Aaron," Daniel said when they were out of the office. "He's inclined to get a little tense. He's not known for spreading joy and light."

She was glad to get outside again and she breathed the hot air with relief. Toby, the shepherd, padded beside them for a little way, then with a sigh, he returned. Courtney looked back at the shed as they reached the corner of the barn. With Toby beside him, Aaron stood deep in the shadows of the doorway, watching them.

She heard Daniel's lighthearted chatter as background music to her thoughts. The pair peered into the gloom of the barn, which once had housed Rockhurst's horses and now held the maroon station wagon, and the pickup "when it's running." There was also a red truck towering over her head. Not a truck, Daniel informed her, a tractor. She was a city girl and thought a tractor was a farm machine.

"The engine that pulls a semi trailer is called a tractor, too. In our case, the tractor pulls a logging rig."

"It's a whole new world up here," she said. "I guess I've just had Lesson One." No, she thought, she'd had Lesson One back there in that small dark office when Aaron had made it clear that he wanted her out of here, wanted her out so much he would lie about Sarah's feelings. He was a confusing man. Or was it only her reaction to him that was complex and uncertain? Thank goodness there was Daniel, with his bright casual manner, to keep things smooth. As she turned to smile at him, he slipped his arms around her, lightly, easily, as if it were the most natural thing in the world, no more meaningful than his way of addressing her.

"Listen to me," he said gravely. "If there's anything you need to know, anything you want...if there's anything I can do, anytime, anyplace, you let me know, you hear?"

"Thank you. I will." Feeling herself blush with pleasure, she turned quickly away. She didn't think Daniel was going to be one more complication, but just in case, she would avoid encouraging him.

He resumed his lighthearted manner as he pointed out the rise behind the buildings. Beyond that, he said, on the north slope, was the stand of trees they were cutting now.

"You can usually hear the engine of the pickup at the cut, or the whine of a saw, but they've shut down for today. Burned-out engine."

They circled the house, and from the front lawn, Daniel showed her where the county road passed, about a mile directly below them. From the lawn several paths led into the deep woods around the house Beyond the deep ravines, which were filled with pine and fir, more gray green mountains rose. And farther yet into the haze caused by the heat were snow-capped ridges. The snow was ragged and patchy at the end of a long summer, but stubbornly holding on. All around the house and the clearing where Courtney and Daniel stood were towering trees. They crowded in on the house, pushing ever nearer, she felt. The house and the people who lived there would have to be vigilant, always on the lookout lest the trees swallow them up and reclaim the mountain.

As they walked the path through an abandoned rose garden, Daniel talked charmingly about himself, about Sarah and Jenny, and about Rockhurst. She was grateful to him for making her feel less nervous and out of place. It wasn't until later, when he had gone back to work and she was back in the house, that she realized he had never mentioned Aaron after that one brief comment. Or Jacob, or the reason she was at Rockhurst. Well, she thought, they could all choose to ignore the subject if they wished. She would not forget why she was there.

CHAPTER THREE

COURTNEY'S DECISION to take the job surprised no one, and she herself wondered if all her doubts and misgivings had been just window dressing in her mind. Perhaps she had known from the moment she saw the elaborately ornamented house in its silent woods that she would stay.

She soon began what became a settled working routine. Breakfast was at the kitchen table, a hearty country offering of eggs and bacon, toast and coffee, plunked down by Jenny on the bare, scrubbed pine table and eaten alone because everyone kept different hours. Lunch was in the sitting room with Sarah, and dinner at the massive mahogany table with the whole family herded together.

Her first problem had been finding a place to work. Jenny suggested an alcove in the front parlor, one of the architectural oddities of the house. Jutting out from the far end of the room was an exaggerated bay window, big enough to hold a pair of armchairs and a pie crust table with its supply of cloisonné vases and bowls. A long mohair sofa stood facing into the room, its back to the alcove, effectively shutting it off. But the furnishings were all wrong for the hours of list-making and reference reading she'd be doing, and with regret, Courtney rejected the alcove.

There seemed to be no suitable place for her work. Sarah used the little sitting room all the time, Daniel seemed to be in and out of the library several times a day, and of course Jenny and Floyd were everywhere. She resigned herself to the prospect of trudging up and down stairs to her room for the next month. But when Aaron heard of her problem, he said, "Put your materials in the alcove. It'll be a good place to work. Lots of light once you clear out the jungle growth of ferns." His flat black eyes dared her to refuse.

Was he ordering her to work there? She quivered inwardly with indignation. His dark gaze held hers for a moment as she used all her strength to hide her feelings. She seemed unable even to talk to him without getting angry. At least she supposed it was anger she felt. Every time he looked at her, she became confused and irritable. It was because he didn't want her here and made no attempt to hide his feelings, she knew, but she would not let him see how he affected her. She wouldn't give him the satisfaction. Coolly she said she would find a place to work as she got to know the house better.

The next morning, however, as she came into the parlor to start on her listings, Aaron was just placing a chair in the bay. It was a straight-backed chair with the seat and back upholstered in needlepoint, a floral wreath against a pale pink background. The chair's proportions looked ideal for the long hours of sitting she would be doing. In place of the armchairs and the delicate tea table was a dainty writing desk, with cabriole legs and gold leaf trim. In spite of its fragile appearance, it was as sturdy as an old-fashioned library table. Across the top was a row of cubby-holes, and in the center was a locking drawer deep enough to hold several of her notebooks. The ferns were gone from the windows, and now the bay was bathed in a soft, clear northerly light.

"If you're determined to stay," Aaron said, pushing the chair in under the writing table, "the least we can do is make it possible for you to do so in reasonable comfort."

Perhaps it was a bribe, she thought, meant to soothe her and put her off guard. Or perhaps he was just making sure she worked where he could keep an eye on her from the shed door a few hundred feet across the yard from the bay window. She looked with longing at the little desklike table, the sensible chair, and the small bookcase where Aaron had already stacked some of her reference books. She resisted the temptation to toss her head and say, "No, thank you." Deciding that the better part of valor was common sense, she transferred all her papers and books to the alcove, locking her notebooks away in the center drawer, and accepted the alcove without further question. Whatever Aaron's motives, the move suited her perfectly.

The days fell into a smooth routine. Aaron and Daniel were out of sight most of the day—mercifully, Courtney thought—rising before dawn and leaving the house before she came downstairs. Aaron was supervising the logging at the cut several miles into the woods, and whatever Daniel's duties were, they kept him out of the house a good deal. It was an indication of the household's peculiar kind of poverty amid riches that neither Daniel nor Aaron owned a car, and since the pickup was seldom in working order, everyone shared the use of the Chevy station wagon.

Sarah came down late each day, dressed with the same care as on the day Courtney arrived. Usually they lunched together, and Courtney would describe what she had been working on during the morning. Sometimes she told Sarah that a particular piece was rare, or was ordinary, but she was careful not to mention possible prices. Mr. Broberg had taught her not to talk money before a sale. It was so easy for the hint of one item's value to set an owner's imagination soaring to heights impossible for the rest of the collection to equal.

Sarah followed Courtney's progress with the keenest interest. She remembered the circumstances around many of Jacob's purchases, and this often helped Courtney to place and appraise the piece. After lunch Courtney put in another two or three hours among the dusty cluttered shelves before she quit. When she had cleaned up—the one thing Jacob had installed unstintingly was modern plumbing—she'd spend another hour or two with reference books and price guides.

Dinners were tense times, with Aaron and Daniel teetering on the raw edge of polite behavior, and both of them turning baleful accusing eyes on Sarah at the most innocent remark. Jenny's cooking leaned heavily to pot roast from the freezer, or chicken bought from the farmer's wife who came around twice a week with eggs and freshly killed hens. The chicken was certainly fresher than any Courtney had ever had in the city, but Jenny's imagination, or skill, never took it beyond a stew, with the addition or absence of dumplings the only variation.

Dinner was early and so was bedtime, which came as a relief to Courtney. There was no television this far up in the mountains and little attempt at sociability. Most evenings Aaron bolted for the office as soon as he was released from the ordeal of dinner. But twice during the week a car drove up the long curving drive, tooted its horn imperiously, and Aaron left. Daniel's glance slid across to Courtney the first time it happened, as Sarah twittered, "That's Samantha, Winston's cousin. She's up from the city."

"And making her usual play for Aaron," Daniel commented.

"Why not?" Sarah said, smiling. "He's young and handsome, and he owns all the land Rockhurst is on. You're just jealous because no rich young blonde is chasing you."

"I'm not interested in rich young blondes." As he answered, his eye was on Courtney, and he grinned when she blushed.

It was true she was only too happy to play gin with him, or listen to records, or even dance a bit to music from the static-ridden radio in the evening. For even Sarah, who chattered away to Courtney at lunch, grew quiet when the others were around. Courtney was always pleased to see Daniel, but she reminded herself that she didn't intend to get interested in anyone again—it was too painful. And she didn't care how many rich blondes picked Aaron up. The ache she felt when Aaron excused himself and left in response to that vulgar honking was nothing more than feminine curiosity. Nothing more. It angered her that Aaron was so implacably set against her being here. But that was her only interest in him. On the whole, she preferred loneliness to involvement.

She had to admit that if loneliness was her preference, there was plenty of it at Rockhurst. Loneliness surrounded the whole house like a fog, slipping between two people and cutting them off, creeping into a room and laying its damp hand on everything. She met it coming down the empty silent corridors and heard it sighing in the trees at night. Loneliness, and the constant friction with Aaron and Daniel, had had its effect on Sarah.

Courtney thought her own mother must have been lonely like that sometimes, with her father so wrapped up in his work, constantly buying new supplies—more canvas, more oils—going off on field trips "to see, to observe." And charging the expense. She remembered how he had shut himself in the studio for long hours while she learned to get her own lunch and bandage her own skinned knees. Yes, Courtney thought, her mother must have been very lonely at times, and forlornly she hoped there had been someone to sit through an evening and listen to her talk about her favorite subjects.

And she hoped her mother's favorite subjects, whatever they were, had been more diversified than Sarah's. For Sarah had only two: Jacob's collection, which seemed to have become as great an obsession with her since his death as it had been with him; and the movies of the forties. In that first week, while Courtney worked on her needlepoint Chinese landscape, Sarah told her the plot of every Ann Sheridan movie, the cast of every Betty Grable movie, and the words to every Alice Faye song.

Courtney would excuse herself about ten, and by the time she was in bed and had read a page or two of her Plantagenet novel, she'd fall asleep—at least for an hour or two. For she woke up at least once each night, frozen in terror, straining every fiber of her body to listen—only to realize that it was the forest quiet that had awakened her.

When she had identified the silence, she could once again hear the sounds that filled the dark. For she soon knew that the forest nights were not really silent at all, but teeming with the noises of the night creatures: an owl in the woods, a branch dropping from a fir tree, Toby occasionally exchanging views with a dog miles away. And always there was the constant rustle of the trees, like a surf whispering urgent secrets to the shore. Sometimes she would lie there, half hearing the night sounds, and think of Sarah, alone here with her family: Daniel, who was young and impatient, and Aaron, who made no attempt to disguise his hostility toward everyone at Rockhurst.

Often Courtney went over in her mind all the places where Jacob might have come by surprise upon a hidden fortune. To find the treasure before anyone could steal it away from Sarah, to be able to protect her, to change the woman's legacy from a few thousand dollars to hundreds of thousands—and make her own name in the art world at the same time—this was the half plan, half fantasy that lulled her back to sleep.

With the early hours and Jenny's wholesome food, Courtney was living an exemplary life except for the matter of exercise. She found it ridiculous to think that city living offered more chance to walk—her favorite mode of exercise—than country life, and she decided to spend part of her afternoons out of doors. She would make up the time lost by being more efficient and by working on her books in the evening. Pleased with her plan, she asked Sarah if there were any especially nice trails nearby, and was surprised to find Sarah clearly upset by the whole idea.

"My dear, you have so much work to do, how can you take time just to go for a walk?" She seemed personally offended. "Surely you'll not finish within the month at that rate."

Courtney thought perhaps the cost of her time was bothering Sarah and hastened to assure her that she planned to walk on her own time. This seemed to upset Sarah even more.

"Oh, my dear, I didn't mean to question your charges. Oh, my, what must you think of me?" She reached across the lunch table and patted Courtney's hand. "My goodness, dear, of course you must take some time for yourself. Time to relax and enjoy yourself. I wasn't for one moment questioning your time-keeping, believe me."

It took Courtney a while to convince Sarah that she believed her.

"It's just that. . . I do so want to have this inventory done with and the sale arranged as quickly as possible. But there—" she shook her head, erasing all objections to Courtney having time off "—I'm just a selfish old woman. You just take all the time you need. You aren't to worry about my foolishness. Promise me you'll forget all about this. Promise?"

She waited until Courtney nodded, then added, "After all, if the sale is one month or the next, what could that matter?"

But Courtney hadn't forgotten Sarah's strange comment when she'd first arrived, about everything changing in a month. So, thoroughly wrapped in guilt, and harboring a tinge of resentment for which she also felt guilty, she left the house at the stroke of three that afternoon. Because she was stealing time from an old woman who perhaps didn't have much time to spare, she tried to rationalize her desire to get out of doors. Perhaps, she told herself, Jacob's treasure was outside somewhere. There were acres— miles—of Rockhurst property. If she found some clue that led to the discovery of the hidden hoard, her time would have been more than well spent.

She followed the twisting drive to the county road, then turned up the road toward the summit. And Jacob Padgett's treasure slipped from her thoughts. The Cascade Mountains never failed to bring to her mind the pioneers who had crossed them blindly, following the only markers, the wagon ruts of those who'd crossed before them. In her imagination she was back with the gold seekers and the religious outcasts, and she turned off onto a logging road that led farther into the woods, supposing it to be a shortcut to the golden shores of California.

It was a shock when a living voice from the present said, "Good afternoon. Are you lost, by any chance? Or perhaps merely misplaced?"

The wagon and oxen of her imagination disappeared in a blink, and she saw a tall handsome man, probably in his fifties, dressed in immaculate country tweeds, leaning indolently against a stone pillar. The pillar was one of a pair framing a short drive to a low, elaborately rustic house. Beyond the gateway, the road she was on dwindled to a pair of ruts.

Embarrassed and panicky, her first instinct was to run. The man didn't look as if he'd exert himself to chase her. An instant later she chided herself for being a fool. He was still standing at ease, smiling, waiting for a civil answer.

"I'm sorry," she said. "Is this your private drive? I thought I was on a logging road."

"Indeed you are. Or were. It was a logging road until I bought this little patch of woods for myself." He roused himself enough to come forward, looking at her with frank curiosity. "I'm Winston Coe. Perhaps Mrs. Padgett has mentioned me. And you, of course, are the young lady from the auction house."

"Art dealer," she corrected him automatically, her mind busy thinking that this was not really a stranger, but Sarah's pet, who made her giggle because he was "wicked." And whose cousin drove an expensive-sounding sports car and pursued men in it.

"Yes, of course. 'Art dealer.' Though you do hold auctions, don't you? And that's how you'll dispose of poor Jacob's gleanings."

"Yes, it is," she said bristling. "That's what Mrs. Padgett wants." She turned and started back down the road. Let him be wicked at someone else's expense.

"Oh, now, don't go all huffy on me." He was at her side and put a hand on her arm. "Please, I promise not to make one more remark that could possibly offend you or, indeed, anyone else."

His smile was amused, and the cocked eyebrow said, wasn't she being just a little bit silly? He touched slender fingers to the yellow ascot, in perfect folds, tucked into the neck of his brown tweed jacket. "You haven't even told me your name. I ought at least to know who it is I've wounded."

She gave in and told him her name.

"I know the Broberg Galleries well. Actually, it was I who recommended them to Sarah. But I must say, Rudi's kept you well hidden."

Yes, she thought, hidden in the back room. She wondered how often Winston Coe had been in the gallery while she was covered with the dust of reference books and packing crates. She looked at the leather elbow patches on his jacket and the walking stick he carried, which completed the picture of a gentleman on a rustic weekend. A weekend should have been enough time in the country for him, she thought, but apparently he—and his cousin?—stayed most of the summer. Sarah had said Winston used to come and talk to Jacob about his collections. Perhaps Winston had some idea of what had so excited Jacob the year before he died.

Before she could frame a question that wouldn't be too abrupt, he invited her into what he termed "the cottage" for a cool drink. In the red dust of the road, with the sun striking the back of her neck and the tops of her shoulders above her boat-neck T-shirt, nothing could have been more welcome. And perhaps she would finally get to see his cousin.

From the carefully laid green stone path that led to a huge double door, hand carved in a pattern of Indian totem figures, to the twenty-five-foot pool off the terrace, there was nothing modest about "the cottage." She couldn't decide whether his calling it that was an attempt to play down its obvious luxuriousness, a bit of inverted snobbishness, or whether it was intended to be amusing.

The pool was like a forest grotto, fed by a splashing waterfall and decked with redwood, its stone sides planted with ferns and trailing wild strawberry. Courtney and Winston looked out on it through floor-to-ceiling windows that made up one wall of a living room done in what Courtney decided could only be called "very rich informal." It was furnished with suede chairs and cowhide rugs and the floors were of cedar planks. It should have looked like a cross between Disneyland, a rodeo and a Playboy club; instead, she thought with approval, it looked luxurious and natural.

She sank into a beige suede chair that was hand stitched to a shape that wrapped around her like a security blanket. At the bar, which stretched between the living room and dining area, Winston Coe mixed her a Tom Collins—against his better judgment, he said, wincing.

Carrying her drink and his own Scotch and water to a small parquet table, he sat down opposite her and said, "Do you like it?"

"Your house? It's lovely—as you must know."

"Yes. But not to everyone's taste. Too stark for some."

"Yes, well, everyone isn't living here. Good taste and beauty cross all preference lines, don't you think?"

"Educated preferences, yes. But the world is full of those who prefer three-piece matched suites."

She laughed, "And whose opinions you happily—and rightly—ignore."

He smiled and she felt warmed by his approval. Sarah was right—the old boy was a wicked snob, but he was rather charming, and she liked him.

"You're admiring my Hallman," he said, following her gaze to a six-foot, very modern painting, a medley of arrows and triangles in blues and greens.

"I was wondering if it really could be a Hallman, to tell you the truth. Way out here? In a temporary home? A summer place, I mean."

"But you see, while I'm here, it is my home. I couldn't spend two months out here without some of my things around me." His hand cut a graceful arc, indicating a small bronze wolf, some leather-bound books, another painting.

Another one obsessed with his art treasures, his possessions, she thought.

"I write, you know," he went on. "Small pieces only, for a rather specialized audience. On art and literature."

He hadn't built this house on what he made writing for art magazines, she thought. Perhaps someone else had made the money—his father, probably.

"It helps my writing to have a few good pictures around me. I have an absolutely irrational fear that without something to use as...a touchstone, so to speak, I would simply lose my feeling, my own touch for beauty and excellence."

"You don't believe that."

"I told you it was irrational." He lifted his glass with an amused smile. "Anyway, I bring up a few pieces to enjoy alone in the peace and quiet of the woods." He got up and crossed the room to a bookshelf along the cedar wall. "A few first editions, a painting or two. Some little piece of sculpture." He handed her a morocco-bound, gold-tooled copy of *Far from the Madding Crowd*. She flipped to the title page and saw it was a first edition.

"Hardly Hardy country up here, of course," Winston said, taking the book from her and placing it carefully on the shelf. He sank back into his chair. "Still, the closed society is much the same." The mischief that had made Sarah giggle shone in his eyes. "Everyone knows everyone else, and most of them are related. It causes some frightful tangles in affairs of the heart." He sipped his drink. "And in money matters, too."

It was obvious he was leading up to something, but she couldn't see what. "Are the Padgetts...they aren't related to everyone."

His face was a mask of secret amusement. "But of course they are. Some of them, at any rate." He set his glass down, as if he had come to a conclusion—or found out something to his satisfaction. "Well, mustn't gossip, must we?"

"No. No, of course not," she said, taken aback. Why had he suddenly changed his mind? What had she revealed? She decided she wasn't going to worry about it. They weren't going to gossip, he said, and apparently she was not going to meet his rich blond cousin after all. But just as she had given up, Winston got to his feet and said, "But you must meet

Samantha,'' then crossed to a doorway leading from the big living-room area.

In answer to his summons, a woman came in and draped herself over one of the chairs. She was everything Courtney had imagined: tawny as a lioness and trim as a panther. After the introductions she prowled around the room until Winston gave her a tall Scotch and water. She scarcely seemed to listen as Winston talked about Courtney's job at Rockhurst, but her eyes flickered when Courtney mentioned Aaron's fixing her a place to work. Courtney was reminded of her cat, Maynard, pretending not to notice as you ran a piece of string by him. . . until he pounced.

''Aaron has always been good to the help,'' Samantha said.

''Really, Samantha!'' Winston rolled his eyes in horror.

''Well, I didn't mean. . .uh, Courtney, is it? I didn't mean she's hired help. . . .''

''Oh, but I am,'' Courtney said coolly, amused. ''Just a hired hand who must be getting back to work.'' She turned to Winston. ''I really must. I came farther than I'd intended. Sarah might begin to worry if I'm gone too long.'' She set her glass down and got up. ''Goodbye, Samantha. I'm so glad to have met you.'' *And I never meant it more,* she thought as Samantha nodded slightly, then closed her eyes, leaning her head back against the suede chair.

Winston followed Courtney to the door and held it open. ''Sarah didn't want you to go out, did she?''

''She didn't say, 'Oh, don't go,' '' she laughed. ''But she didn't urge me out into the fresh air, either. How did you know?''

"Well, don't fret. She's just anxious to get this sale going."

What was the terrible urgency? "Are...I shouldn't ask this, but I can't very well ask the family. Are there creditors breathing down her neck?"

"No, nothing like that, my dear." He took her elbow and came down the path with her. "Here, let me show you a shortcut back, then you won't worry Sarah a minute longer than necessary." They turned away from the county road at the gate and crossed the logging road to a tunnellike path burrowed through the salal and fern that crowded around the feet of the Douglas firs. "Sarah's hurry is more of a *tempus fugit* sort of thing," Winston said. "She feels she's put in her waiting time, and now she's ready to get on with it, so to speak."

"On with what?"

As they went farther into the woods, the light dimmed and the air cooled, filtered by the firs. But the trail was well defined and wide enough at that point for him to walk beside her.

"Get on with living," he said. "Spending forty cents without having to explain it to Jacob."

"But—"

"This path will lead right to the front door of Rockhurst," he cut in. "You'll be perfectly safe; no wild animals around, and a falling limb is the worst danger you'll meet. You'll forgive me for not going all the way with you. My dear cousin has some sort of expedition planned for the balance of the day, I believe, and I dare not disappoint her. She is a devil when crossed."

"You were saying about Sarah... "

"It was nothing, really," he said. "You know, I'm giving a lovely big party soon, and you must come."

She didn't want to talk about parties. She wanted to know about Sarah. "Yes, well. . .I don't know."

"Nonsense. Of course you'll come. I give a bash every year toward the end of the season. People come up from the city and all around. Everyone at Rockhurst is invited." His eyes glinted momentarily as the ever present breeze opened a path for the sun to stream down onto his face. "And, I might add, they all show up." He smiled again. "And so must you. Details later."

"Well, we'll see." She couldn't commit herself until she was sure that Sarah really did go to Winston's parties.

"Remember, it'll give you a chance to escape Jenny's cooking for one evening." He stopped and an arch look widened his eyes. "Oh, shouldn't have said that. I did promise not to offend, but you see how hard it is to avoid all the possibilities."

As she laughed at him, he pointed the way down the path and began to turn back toward his own place. "Off you go, my dear. See you at the party."

In spite of the heat, she hurried along the path toward Rockhurst, the guilty feeling that she had shirked her responsibilities growing stronger the closer she got. By the time she reached the edge of the woods and broke through to the hot dry sun again, she was panting. Across the wide lawn, the house seemed to stare balefully at her from windows encased in carved and ornamented spandrels. A lone raven clung to the highest ornament on top of the tower and watched silently as she neared the house.

In the background the wind hummed its tuneless song, and behind her in the woods, insects droned an alto harmony. Farther up the hill a jay sang a solo.

Suddenly, the wind song was ripped apart by a long piercing scream. The cry came from inside the house, and then was heard again. The raven flapped his wings once and soared away over the forest as Courtney began to run toward Rockhurst.

CHAPTER FOUR

As COURTNEY RAN through the open front door, the family was pouring into the hall from the back of the house. Floyd and Jenny pushed through the kitchen door, and Aaron and Daniel were right behind them. At the foot of the staircase, Sarah lay on the floor, her cheek pressed against the carpet, her arms outstretched and her legs bent under her. She groaned softly, the sound rising to a sharp cry as Jenny, dropping to her knees beside Sarah, tried to lift her head.

"Oh, my God," Jenny moaned. "Down all them steps. Oh, God, what'll we do?" It wasn't a question, but a refrain of dismay.

Aaron knelt beside Jenny and, reaching across her, lifted Sarah's wrist and felt her pulse. Without looking up, he said, "Get a coat, a blanket, anything to cover her with." When Jenny didn't move, Aaron said, "Daniel," and Daniel hurried out through the kitchen. He was back in seconds with a heavy red and black mackinaw, and Aaron laid it gently over Sarah's shoulders and chest. Sarah's eyelids fluttered, and Aaron murmured something to her. He moved her arms to her sides and straightened her legs, each to an accompanying moan.

Everyone else stood by helplessly, watching as Aaron felt Sarah's shoulders and ribs, then her legs and arms. Sarah's eyes followed his hands with a worried look, but except for the quiet moaning that escaped her throat, she said nothing.

At last Aaron sat back and said. "Nothing broken, as far as I can tell. You may be bruised some." He moved aside to let Jenny put her rolled-up apron under Sarah's head. "What happened?"

"I was looking. . . ." Sarah stopped, her eyes wide. She looked almost pleadingly at Aaron.

"What were you looking for?"

She moved her head slightly until she found Courtney in the group gathered around her. The blue-shadowed lids closed slowly.

"Nothing. It's all right. I just . . . tripped."

Courtney stood rooted with horror. Sarah had been looking for her—and because she wasn't there, Sarah had fallen down that long flight of stairs. Swimming in a sea of guilt and remorse, she struggled to catch her breath.

Aaron looked away from Sarah and asked Jenny to get her bed ready. His eyes passed over Daniel and Courtney, who were standing together, waiting, then flicked back to Courtney. "She may want something after she's settled," he said. Courtney prepared to wait in the front hall.

"I'll take you up in a minute," he said, bending closer to Sarah and brushing away one of the gray curls that had fallen onto her forehead. "You tripped?" he asked.

"Yes. I must have."

"From where? Where were you?"

"At the top of the stairs."

Aaron looked up at the staircase curving away

above his head. He looked back at Sarah, then at the stairs again, and Sarah flinched. With his face close to hers, his voice low, he said, "Damn you, Sarah Padgett, you scared the life out of us. I hope next time you really do fall downstairs."

Courtney caught her breath and felt her stomach lurch. It was as if he had struck her. She had never heard anyone speak that way to another person. Neither she nor Daniel could say a word.

In the silence, Sarah whimpered and clutched at his hand, but he shook her off and stood up.

"Aar...on...."

Ignoring her, he turned and began to walk away. Daniel reached out and stopped him.

"What the hell's the idea? Talking to her like that!" He blocked Aaron's way.

"The idea is, I refuse to play the scene as written. Remorseful family, hovering devotedly."

"You bastard, she could have been killed."

"Think so? Then go attend to the stricken heroine. I've had enough." He brushed past Daniel, then stopped and turned back to Courtney. "You were the first one through the front door?"

"Yes. No, I couldn't have been. At least, the door was standing open."

Aaron's face twisted in a bitter smile. "Of course." He turned to Sarah. "Making sure the rest of the players heard their cues, were you?" He strode out of the house and slammed the door.

Sarah cried softly, and Daniel made a move to follow Aaron. Courtney stopped him.

"She needs you. That's more important."

Daniel hesitated, leaning toward the door, then

pulled himself up. "You're right." He clenched his fists. "But I'd like to...." He turned to Floyd. "Well, don't just stand there. Let's get her upstairs."

Courtney wanted to protest against moving her before a doctor had seen her, but she knew the nearest doctor must be miles away. Then, as Daniel and Floyd hovered awkwardly over her, offering clumsy hands, Sarah got to her feet. Her hand trembled as she reached for the railing, and she looked with dismay at the long staircase. With a glance at Daniel, Floyd shrugged, then scooped Sarah up in his arms and carried her up the stairs.

When Sarah had been propped up in her bed on an elaborate arrangement of pillows, surrounded by her flirting fans and Dresden dancers, Jenny ordered everyone else out of the room. Courtney welcomed the chance to be alone and think about what had just happened. She shut herself in her room and sat staring out the window at the restless firs, trying to make sense out of Aaron's actions. She didn't understand his reference to audiences and cues. He might have been speaking to Sarah in a code that only they understood. But whatever the language, the brutality was clear. There was no mistaking the fact that he had verbally attacked a helpless and possibly injured woman and had left her in tears.

It wasn't until dinner that Courtney saw either of "the boys" again. The "bank-night china" and assorted silverware were laid out as usual on a tablecloth that was clean but so worn the wood of the table showed through in places. Jenny had found time to stew another chicken with carrots and peas from the garden, and it was clear that life was going on as usual.

Resentment flared up in Courtney. It was as if no one had paid any attention to Sarah's fall down the stairs. Dropping any pretense of staying out of things as a guest or hired help—whichever she was—should do, she asked them what they thought had caused Sarah's accident.

"Has she fallen before?" she asked, determined to force them to discuss it.

Daniel laid his fork down and looked more serious than she had yet seen. "No, but she's old, not as strong as she used to be, whether she admits it or not." With an air of dismissal, he attacked his plate again.

Eager to keep him on the subject, she said, "Maybe. I mean, she does seem frail, but she's not really that old. And she must know every step, every thread of the carpet so well. She said...she said she was looking for something. I suppose she wasn't paying attention." She turned to Aaron, who didn't seem to be listening. "Is that what happened, do you suppose?"

"Sarah is not a careless type. Not paying attention to where she's going...is not her style." His dark eyes still held a simmering anger.

She stared across the table at him as he helped himself to more chicken stew. How could he be so cold and heartless? But you could tell by looking at him, she thought. Hard and strong. A man with no patience for weakness, or for subterfuge. A man who knew what he wanted and was willing to go after it. But what was it he wanted? She blushed as he looked up and caught her eye.

"I'm sorry if you think I'm unsympathetic." His

eyebrows appeared to shrug. "But Sarah often causes her own problems." The merest hint of a smile crossed his face. "But then, don't we all?"

She restrained herself from commenting that he must have been one of Sarah's problems, and that his grandmother hadn't brought that on herself. "What I don't understand is your lack of concern." It took an effort to keep her tone civil. "She might have been seriously hurt."

He put his hands flat on the table and leaned across it toward her. "She might have been hurt falling downstairs. But she wasn't."

With vindictive glee, she saw that she had succeeded in irritating him.

He added slowly with exaggerated enunciation, "She wasn't hurt because she didn't fall."

"I don't think it's a joking matter," she snapped.

"Oh, you weren't intended to take it as a joke." He smiled as if to himself and again began to eat.

Clanging his coffee cup against his saucer, Daniel said, "All right, what do you think happened?"

"I think she faked the whole thing. She may have tripped on the last step or two. Or, more likely, she just arranged herself at the bottom."

Courtney stared at him in disbelief.

"Oh, come on, Aaron." Daniel looked pained. "She said—"

"She said she fell—or tripped—from the top," Aaron said. "From the top, mind you." He gestured with his fork. "Of that long, curving staircase. But there wasn't a mark on her."

"Would a couple of broken ribs have made you happier?" Daniel said. "Why would she do a thing like that anyway, for Pete's sake?'' But Courtney noticed that a note of acceptance had crept into his voice.

''Why do you think? I don't know what the connection is, but you can bet it's got something to do with getting her hands on the cash.''

But if that was true, Courtney knew what the connection was. Sarah's message had been, *I was looking for you and you weren't there. And that's what caused me to fall.*

''I don't see how pretending to fall downstairs is going to help her get the money any sooner,'' Daniel said.

But don't you see? Courtney thought. *If it's true, it means Sarah is trying to get me to stay in and work in the afternoon and not waste time roaming around in the forest.* If it were true, which Courtney didn't believe for a moment. She agreed when Daniel said, ''I think you're being too hard on the old girl.''

Aaron shrugged. ''Could be. I've been wrong before.''

Courtney could almost hear him adding in his mind: but not often. Well, he must have been wrong this time. Sarah couldn't have gone to such lengths just to convince Courtney that there was no time for afternoon walks. That was just the sort of motive Aaron would think of. A liar distrusts everyone's word, and a thief suspects everyone of stealing. What was Aaron, she wondered, that he would suspect poor Sarah of such deceit? Not that Courtney wouldn't have liked to believe it, for it would have removed the cloud of guilt that hung over her. But she knew better. Aaron was just coldhearted and brutal.

"Real or not," Aaron was saying, "Sarah's fall has her boxed in her bedroom for a couple of days. She's got to play the scene through to the end." Again the eyebrow went up. "I stopped in before dinner, and already she was lonesome."

He actually looked amused, Courtney thought in outrage.

"She said you had promised to read to her later," he went on to Daniel. "That's good because I'm going to be tied up with the quarterly reports tonight."

And leave poor rich Samantha all alone all evening? Courtney thought cattily. What a shame. She kept her eyes on her plate, hoping she wasn't developing a sudden turn toward spite, complete with claws and fangs.

Daniel protested, "I didn't tell Sarah any such thing."

Aaron accepted that without surprise. "Well, you know Sarah." At this Courtney looked up and caught Aaron's glance. He explained, "Sarah tends to think that if she says a thing, that makes it so. I suppose having someone read to her is what she hoped would happen."

"Well, I can't do it. I've got to go back and see that logger again, over at Snoquilicum," Daniel said. "The one that's got the used tractor for sale."

Aaron looked at him. "I see. And are you meeting him at Jilly's Tavern? They must have missed you lately."

Always ready to do battle with Aaron, Courtney thought there was nothing wrong with Daniel's going to the local bar. Still, she didn't believe Daniel was the type to spend a lot of time at a place like that, drinking beer and dancing with the local girls. He had hardly left Rockhurst in all the time she'd been there. Then a new thought occurred to her. Perhaps he was staying in because *she* was there. It was a flattering thought, but not a comfortable one.

"Just don't forget," Aaron was advising Daniel about the tractor, "you can arrive at a figure, but there isn't any money available right now."

Daniel glared. "You think I don't know that?"

Partly in an effort to avoid the start of another quarrel, Courtney broke in. "I'll look in on Sarah. I'd be glad to read to her." She didn't add that she thought it might ease her conscience.

"There won't be much else to entertain you around here tonight—unless you were going with Daniel."

"Now, there's a good idea," Daniel said, grinning. "How about it, Courtney?"

Aaron was sneering at her ability to adjust to the quiet life of the country, she supposed, and to amuse herself without Daniel's help. And he had no right to do that. Besides, she'd go with Daniel if she wanted to, whether he liked it or not. "I was going to go over my lists." She spoke through teeth clenched in anger.

"Really. Working day and night, are you? You must want to get this job over with as soon as possible."

"I had planned to take a little time in the afternoons, if you must know, to...get out, get a little air." Why was she explaining to him? "But now...."

"You're not sure you should? I see." He seemed taken aback. His gaze seemed to go right through to her innermost thoughts. "Of course you should take a break in the afternoon. What are we running here, a sweatshop?"

"Well, it just seemed. . . ." Her voice trailed off, lost in the silence of the dining room. Even the clatter of dishes from the kitchen had stopped. She shrank back in her chair.

Aaron's voice was soft and low. For the first time, it lacked the anger and menace it usually held. "My dear child, if you don't look after yourself, no one will." Then the anger returned. "Certainly no one around here." His face was impassive as he added, "You'll probably work that much more efficiently because of a bit of change. As for this evening, I'm sure Sarah would rather you got on with your work instead of stopping to entertain her."

He was right, of course; she should work. Still. . . . "Maybe when I've finished," she said. "It might be pretty late, but I could look in."

"If you want to." He sounded disinterested. "But don't worry about it. One evening alone won't hurt her."

Courtney's heart sank. Just when Aaron was showing a glimmer of being nice—a little concern for her, a little sympathy for Sarah—he turned hard and cold again. No doubt that was his true nature, and the moments of kindness were mistakes, slipups that let a touch of warmth get through that icy soul.

IT WAS AFTER ELEVEN that night before she found, in one of her reference books, the mark of the little-known potter that was incised on the bottom of the Staffordshire piece she was researching. As she put everything away, rubbing the back of her neck and stretching, she thought she would just go very quietly to look in on Sarah, guiltily hoping she'd find her already asleep. But as she walked down the hall, Courtney saw with resignation that Sarah's door was open and light streamed out onto the flowered carpet. Then she heard voices.

"Read it just once more," Sarah was saying, her thin voice a whisper of flute notes in the dark house.

"You silly old woman, I've read it to you twice already," Aaron said with a chuckle

"I know, but it's just a short poem."

"Short!"

"Well, it's not awfully long. And I like the way you read it. I can just picture Errol Flynn as the Highwayman. And Olivia de Havilland as the landlord's daughter, of course."

"Olivia de Havilland isn't black-eyed."

"She is too."

"I think you see yourself."

"Don't be smart-alecky. Read it once more."

Courtney could tell by the tone of her voice that Sarah was settling back against the pillows and perhaps pulling the comforter up against her cheek. Courtney was just about to tiptoe away when a change in Aaron's voice stopped her.

"If I read it again, you've got to promise me something," he said. "You've got to let that child have a moment or two to herself."

"Oh, but Aaron—"

"No buts about it, you old slave driver. You can't expect her to stay cooped up in this house twenty-four hours a day working over your art goods."

Courtney stopped in the middle of the stairs, her hand clutching the railing as she realized Aaron was talking about her.

"Well, it's her job. Besides—" Sarah's voice took on a sly note "—why are you so interested?"

Courtney held her breath, straining to hear his answer.

"Simple humanity, Sarah. The child is not a slave. If you're not careful, you'll have the state labor relations department down on you for cruel treatment of employees. Simple humanity, nothing more. But I want you to promise to behave yourself."

Courtney began to breathe again, but was discomfited by how disappointed she felt. She couldn't understand why she should feel this way. Surprise she could understand, surprise that he would make an effort on behalf of someone else. But why should she feel let down? Fatigue, probably, she decided. It had been a long and eventful day. As she tiptoed away, she heard Aaron's voice began softly, " 'The wind was a torrent of darkness among the gusty trees....' "

Hardly knowing what she expected, or why she was doing it, Courtney went back downstairs and waited in her little bay window for Aaron to come down. She knew he made the rounds, checking doors and turning out lights the last thing each night, and it wasn't long before she heard his footsteps on the stairs. Nervously she sat in the semidarkness of the front parlor, her knees shaky, her hands icy cold. There was no need for all this shyness, she told herself firmly. All she wanted to do was thank him for his concern, and he could hardly rebuff her for that.

But she knew in her heart he could. After all, she had never been anything but snippy and cool to him. Why would he expect a friendly gesture from her now?

She was not disappointed. As he came into the room, she could see him give a little start of surprise. Then, as if gathering his wits together, he said, "Well, waiting up for Daniel, are you?"

"Certainly not." She got to her feet and crossed the room in quick angry strides. She told herself it was ridiculous to be hurt and annoyed because this oaf chose to misunderstand why she was here. "I came to thank you for standing up for me." She snapped the words at him. "I just happened to overhear you. I was not listening—Sarah's door was open, and I couldn't help hearing. Thank you." She glowered at him.

He looked amused and stood his ground in the doorway, blocking what should have been her grand exit.

"You are most welcome. For such gracious thanks as that, I'd go to any amount of trouble." Even in the dim light coming from her desk across the room, Courtney could see he was trying not to laugh.

"Well, I'm sorry. But you did come in with your snide remark about waiting for Daniel. And I had meant to say thank-you a little more nicely, I guess."

"You guess." His eyes had lost their opaque blackness and seemed bottomless in their depth.

She laughed. "Well, yes. A little." She looked into black eyes that seemed to be fairly twinkling and laughed aloud. "But probably only a little." She started to turn back to her desk.

"That's the first time I've seen you laugh," he said quietly. "It's lovely."

Surprised, she turned back to look up at him and found his arms around her, his head bent over her. One strong hand slipped up to the back of her head, holding her prisoner while his lips sought hers. His other arm held her tightly, and she felt as if she might melt away or crumble into dust in the heat of his embrace. Only the strength of his arms kept her from falling.

In an instant it was over. He released her and stepped back, leaving her reeling against the door jamb. "I'm sorry." His growl seemed to be forced from the depths of his being. "I don't.... I'm not as cold as you seem to think me." He drew himself up and stood erect and forbidding before her. "I will try to behave better in the future." With that he turned and strode across the hall and out into the night.

COURTNEY WENT TO HER ROOM prepared to spend a restless night. As she got ready for bed, she turned over in her mind Aaron's actions, and especially his reaction to their kiss. Why all the abject apology? Was it because she was a guest, or hired help—there was that question again—and the master shouldn't take advantage? Or did he really think something had been developing between Daniel and her in this short time? Or was it something to do with himself—a wife and children somewhere that no one had bothered to mention? She climbed into the huge Jacobean bed, ready to examine all the possibilities. Instead, to her great disappointment when she discovered it the next morning, she fell asleep.

As soon as she could the next day, Courtney looked in on Sarah and found her already restlessly churning the bedcovers and punching the pillows, bored with the prospect of a full day in bed. On the other hand, it clearly was not entirely distasteful.

"That Jenny. She just bullies me so," Sarah said, squiggling down into her pillows. "She said if I didn't stay put, she'd call in Dr. Barnes."

No one is ever too old to be babied, Courtney thought, amused at Sarah's obvious pleasure in Jenny's concern.

"But I just cannot stand that old fussbudget doctor," Sarah went on. "I'll not have him around anymore, with his *hmmm-m*ing and his *tsk*ing." She looked like a gray-haired Shirley Temple, pout and all. "So I'll just have to be a good girl, won't I?" She repeated her squiggling movements, then asked Courtney to fetch her a sweater from the big walnut wardrobe, and a deck of cards from the table drawer. "I suppose it would meet with Jenny's approval if I played a little solitaire."

The wardrobe, which reached almost to the carved ceiling molding, had double doors that opened at the front. Inside, hanging in perfect order, Courtney found perhaps a dozen dresses, all of the same decade as the teal blue dress Sarah had worn every evening since Courtney arrived. There were dresses with puffed sleeves, short sleeves, and bracelet-length sleeves, padded shoulders and ruffled peplums. On the shelf above sat a row of hats covered with tiny artificial forget-me-nots and pink sweet peas. Shoes were lined up in neat pairs: black shoes and white ones, pink shoes with ankle straps, and teal blue pumps with little bows at the instep.

"On the right of the top shelf, dear." Sarah's voice interrupted Courtney's fascinated inspection.

Courtney found the sweater Sarah wanted, a white angora gone cream with age, and took it across to her. As she helped Sarah get it on and arranged to her satisfaction, Courtney longed to ask her about all those clothes. They had an air of expectancy about them, like clothes for a trousseau or a vacation, ready to be packed and admired.

She longed, too, to ask Sarah about Aaron. As soon as his name surfaced in her thoughts, she realized it had been there all along at the edge of her mind. She was seized by an urge to talk about him, what he was like, what his attitude was toward women. Of course, she knew about Samantha, and she presumed there were others among the local girls, and perhaps among Winston's city friends. Did Aaron take them all lightly? Was he a kiss-and-run type? She knew that nowadays a kiss meant nothing—at least to most men. People kissed everyone and anyone. They kissed their friends and their co-workers and talk-show hosts they'd never met. And none of those kisses meant anything. She got the deck of cards from the drawer in the little table and slammed it shut, setting a Dresden dancer off on a shaky *pas seul*. Aaron's kiss didn't mean anything to her, either. She glared at the porcelain dancer, daring her to topple over, and when she didn't, Courtney gave a little nod of satisfaction. She would spend no more time and energy thinking about Aaron . . . or his kisses. She wrenched her mind back to what Sarah was saying.

"...And if you wouldn't mind, tell Jenny I'm ready for breakfast."

JENNY JEALOUSLY REFUSED to let Courtney carry the breakfast tray up to Sarah. But when she came back down, she accepted Courtney's renewed offer of help. Jenny had come in complaining that Sarah wanted to be carried down to the front parlor to sit.

"Sitting room ain't good enough. Too small. If she's expecting everybody to gather 'round, clucking over her, she's in for a surprise." Jenny slammed the heavy crockery from the tray into the galvanized iron sink. "Parlor's a mess."

Courtney's sense of guilt over Sarah's fall deepened as she realized how much extra work Jenny would be doing, and she offered to help.

After a moment's hesitation, Jenny agreed with resignation that she could use a hand and led the way into the parlor. "You can start on those lamps behind the sofa." She tossed Courtney a dust cloth. "Don't suppose you ever learned to dust properly," she grumbled. "Don't stir it up. And be careful of the beads." A fringe of tiny glass beads slithered across Courtney's fingers as she ran her hands around the lamp shades.

Jenny began attacking the sofa, pulling the loose cushions off and whacking them with a whisk broom as if they were offending children. The household vacuum, a wheezing upright with no extra attachments, was effective only on the worn carpets; all the other tasks were done the way Courtney's grandmother had done them. Jenny commented bitterly that it was because Courtney had shifted everything around to inspect it that the room was unfit for use.

"In my day, we was taught it wasn't polite to look under the plates and things. Still ain't."

Rather than defend her actions as part of her job, which she figured Jenny knew anyway, Courtney jumped into the opening the housekeeper had given her. In her friendliest tone—speak nicely, her father had said, make them like you—she said cautiously, "Your life has been mostly at Rockhurst, hasn't it? I mean, you've been here a long time."

"Came when Sarah did."

"When she was a bride? How nice."

"No, she wasn't no bride." She took her irritation out on the cushions. "She was the housekeeper. Came to take care of things when Mrs. Padgett, the first, was expecting. Then Anabelle was born, and Mrs. Padgett took the fever and died." She put the cushions back, patted them, and straightened up, staring at them reflectively. "Me and Sarah stayed on. I was just a kid then. Underhousemaid, you might say. Fourteen. And nursemaid, and everything else. As usual."

Things had stayed that way for almost two years, she said. Then Jacob Padgett began to pay court to Sarah, his young housekeeper, and within a few months they were married. It had seemed very romantic to Sarah, and to the still-younger Jenny.

"We should of knowed better, both of us. Wasn't long before I could see he'd married her just to save the salary."

"Oh, Jenny."

"I don't know what else you'd call it. She went on doing all the same work, only she didn't get paid."

Jenny's anger returned, and she assaulted an armchair, crusading against any crumbs that might have escaped. "Not being a blood relation, she didn't even come first with him—baby Anabelle did. But not being hired help, she couldn't just quit and walk out, like she wanted to. He was a mean man, Jacob was. And it wasn't like he was all that interested in—" her voice dropped "—the baser side of marriage."

Courtney marveled that a generation that seldom spoke of "the baser side" always seemed to be aware of everyone's involvement with it.

But Sarah stuck it out, Jenny said, at first because she was in love with the rich older man. Later, her feelings changed, but she stayed anyway.

Again Courtney thought it must have been the way of a different generation, and she both pitied the women who were trapped, and admired them for sticking by their bargains in an unquestioning way that her generation couldn't match.

Jenny's face was hard as a bisque doll's. "She figured she had something coming, and she wasn't about to leave without she got it."

So much for that generation's nobility, Courtney thought.

"And I figured she was right," Jenny went on. "So I stayed with her." Jenny had even given up a marriage proposal to stay and watch out for Sarah. "Jacob had cheated and connived and one way or another done us out of so much that we meant to stay and get what was coming to us." She kept her head down, brushing the skirt of the chair.

There was no happy ending to it all, she said. Jacob wasn't the kind to leave a remembrance to an

old family retainer for almost fifty years of service.
"Any fool should've known that, I guess. Never was
any thanks to be had in this house, and never will
be."

Her bitter tone was a sad comment on her life,
Courtney thought. To be sixty or older and realize
you'd made the wrong choice must be galling. To
find you had devoted your life to. . .what? A dream?
That wouldn't be so bad. Some goal that was beyond
your capacity? At least you could say you'd tried.
But to have given all your years to a thankless, face-
less job. . . . Courtney shuddered.

"Surely Sarah has appreciated your devotion. She
must be grateful to you for standing by her."

"I don't know. I used to think so, but now I'm not
so sure. Money does funny things to people. Before,
when old Jacob was alive, didn't seem as though the
money was real in Sarah's mind." Jenny picked up
the broom and with slow careful strokes began to
sweep down the heavy velvet draperies. "But it's real
enough now. And she's no quicker to part with it
than Jacob was." As her words grew sharper, so did
her strokes, until little clouds of dust rose from the
velvet. "All I want is to get what's mine and get out.
'Cause this house ain't safe."

"Not safe?"

"Something'll happen to her if she's not careful."

"Jenny. .."

"Them boys didn't like having everything split
that way it was, you know. Aaron's got the land and
the timber, but only as a. . .what'd the lawyer call it?
Residue. . .residual, that's it. A residual heir is what
he is. Besides, the timber never has paid. Daniel

wants to develop the land into a vacation place. Condominiums and like that. That's the real reason they fight all the time, in case you didn't know it. And they need their share of the cash before they can do anything one way or the other.''

"I thought everything was left to Sarah.''

"That's what she'll tell you, but it ain't so. She gets two-thirds of everything from the collection, and the Boys split the rest, and when she dies, Aaron gets the land. Like I say, they need that money before they can do anything. All three of 'em.''

"You surely don't think they'd...do anything to her. You can't think....'' It was a fruitless argument, and Courtney stopped herself, because obviously Jenny did think the whole house was full of evil and danger. A glance around at the heavy dark paneling, the windows barricaded against air and sunlight by the velvet hangings, the crazy, almost violent crowding of every space with Jacob's porcelain and glass, made her think that perhaps Jenny was right. Could people live in this oppressive, threatening atmosphere for long without becoming threatening themselves?

CHAPTER FIVE

JENNY REFUSED TO DISCUSS the family any further, and
for a while she and Courtney worked in silence as they
cleaned the front parlor. But Courtney's mind was
never still, and in a moment she remembered Sarah's
strange wardrobe, and she asked Jenny about it.

"You saw the dresses, did you? And the fur jacket?
No? Well, it's there, in back." Jenny's smile was
strangely soft and pitying.

"They look . . . as if they were all bought at the same
time."

"They was, more or less. After the war we was all
fixing to get out of here. Most of us, anyhow." She
stood motionless, holding the broom in front of her.
She half turned from Courtney and gazed out the
window. In profile her face somehow seemed softer.
Webster-Bishop, the lumber people, had leased the
entire east slope, she said, and for once it looked as if
there'd be enough money to leave Rockhurst. Sarah
sent away for her clothes. She wasn't going out of
here barefoot after so many years of working without
pay. Everything was set but a departure date. Jacob
was busy during this time, tracking down anything he
could get out of France or Germany; his sources were
refugees needing money, who were forced to sell their
collections and family heirlooms.

"Or poor souls who'd escaped from Japan or somewheres with some little piece of jade, the only thing they could carry. Oh, the war kept Jacob hopping, all right." Contempt rang in her voice.

Then, she went on, Anabelle, Jacob's only child, ran away to the city. That made Jacob open his eyes and look around. His treatment of Anabelle, when he got her back, was enough to make Sarah think better of trying to leave.

"He didn't like his daughter's going off that way. And he was bound and determined no one else was going to leave him." She shook her head sadly. "We was set to spying and tattling on each other. It got so's you couldn't talk to no one for fear they'd tell Jacob. See, if you didn't tell him something, and later he found out you knew—well, his wrath was terrible. And we was all looking out for Anabelle. On account of her coming home...in the family way."

"She was pregnant?"

"Yes. And not very strong. So we had to...stand between, sort of." Jenny shuddered and turned back to sweeping the rug. "Well, Sarah kept the wardrobe ready, but Jacob wouldn't even take her to Seattle anymore after that, and he never left any money around the house. So she never did get a good enough chance again." She shook her head. "Between one month and the next, things was different."

"You make it sound as if she was a...a prisoner all these years," Courtney objected. "Couldn't she just have run away?"

"Yeah, she could have done that. But not with enough money to live on for more'n a couple of weeks." Jenny fell silent, as if she was thinking it over. "When a body's been poor, really poor, like Sarah was when she was a girl, then you never do have enough money. There just is no such thing as enough money. I guess that's what Sarah was, in a way, a prisoner." She was silent again for a moment. "I guess that's what all of us up here are, one way or another."

Courtney wanted to protest that she was not like the others, not a prisoner of her own emotions and prejudices. But she stopped herself rather than interrupt Jenny.

All the softness had left Jenny's face now, and she shook the draperies into folds again with a vigorous snapping motion. "You could say Sarah was a prisoner on account of not wanting to starve, nor to work, either." Another sharp snap, and the draperies fell into place. "She paid dearly for her security; seems like she might be left to enjoy it. But someone wants to take it away from her." Her voice dropped and she went on, more to herself than to Courtney. "I just want to get something and get out of here. I gotta save what little's left of my life for my own self. If I can help Sarah get out safe, too, that's fine. But if she's gonna get mean and stingy, then she'll just have to look out for herself."

It was a strange relationship, Courtney thought, between Sarah and Jenny. Part love, part contempt; part understanding, part greed.

Suddenly Jenny stopped and turned to face Courtney, looking at her as if just realizing how much she had been talking. Courtney was afraid she had made an enemy by listening to her. Painful experience had taught her that exchanging girlish confidences didn't pave the way to long-lasting friendships, but to ever-lasting suspicion. Perhaps Jenny would always wonder when and to whom Courtney was going to expose her. She longed to reassure Jenny that she hadn't said anything shameful, but she knew it wouldn't make any difference. What mattered wasn't whether secrets were good or bad, but that they were private. Jenny had been willing to tolerate her up to now. Courtney was afraid their relationship would never again be even that good.

And, in exchange, all she had learned was that Jacob had had an only child named Annabelle, there were three beneficiaries to Jacob's will and the proceeds of the sale. And that Jenny wouldn't harm Sarah, would protect her, at least until Jenny received the reward she felt she had coming.

Courtney couldn't bring herself to believe Sarah was in danger—certainly not from one of the Boys. She had raised Aaron...but of course, she was only his stepgrandmother. And Daniel, he was even further removed. Even so, she didn't think they would hurt Sarah. But could she believe they wouldn't steal from her?

Courtney knew it was none of her concern; but Sarah had no one else but Jenny and her. Poor Sarah, who reminded her so much of her own mother. Courtney was determined to do something to help her. She had no idea what, or how; but she would help Sarah.

And, she had to admit, self-interest was a part of it, too. The truth was, she was no better than the rest of them. They were all circling Rockhurst like the ravens, ready to swoop down on any crumb of value in Jacob's legacy and pick it clean.

In spite of the gloom that had descended over Courtney and Jenny, they got the parlor ready at last, and Sarah was enthroned in time to watch Courtney finish her morning's work. At lunch, Sarah treated Courtney to the details of *Seventh Heaven*, that Janet Gaynor version. With the picture of Sarah's rack of dresses fresh in her mind, Courtney found Sarah's absorption in old movies more understandable—and infinitely sad.

By the end of her third week at Rockhurst, Courtney had accumulated a small stack of notes full of questions she couldn't answer. Questions on the value of the brace of pistols in the library, along with two other antique handguns she had found there. Questions on some Italian glass with a mark she couldn't identify, and an especially puzzling piece, a cross that looked like early Celtic work. She needed to look these pieces up in reference books that she hadn't brought with her, but which she knew were available in Seattle.

She tried phoning Mr. Broberg to have him send the books to her. But between the terrible connection, so bad that he could hardly understand which books she was asking for, and his reluctance to let them out of the shop, she gave up that idea and said she would come down for them.

Reluctantly, she broke the news to Sarah, who fulfilled Courtney's worst predictions and became very upset. "It will take you two whole days," she wailed.

"Well, I could try to come back the same day," Courtney said doubtfully.

"Nonsense," Aaron said, striding in from the hall

to the small sitting room where they were talking. "That's too far to drive and then turn right around and come back. It wouldn't be safe."

"This has nothing to do with you," Sarah said regally.

Even though Courtney agreed with Aaron's assessment of the trip, she applauded Sarah's objection. Aaron was just too bossy to put up with.

He turned to glare at Sarah. "You have no idea how long that drive is."

"Really, Aaron. With the new highways—"

"The new highways don't extend up the mountain."

"Well, but—"

"No buts about it. The girl simply can't do everything just as you want it. Don't make her feel guilty because she doesn't kill herself in your service."

"I'm quite capable of deciding whether or not I can drive to Seattle and back, thank you."

"Oh, you're capable of deciding not to make the round trip. But coping with Sarah's attitude is another thing." He turned back to Sarah. "Leave her alone, you hear? Behave yourself."

"Well, I'm sure I didn't mean to intimidate the poor little thing," Sarah said, with a sweet smile for Courtney.

"Of course you didn't." Courtney reached over and touched Sarah's pale hand. "I know that."

"You know nothing of the sort," Aaron put in. "But it doesn't matter, as long as it's understood that she will take two days, or more if she wants it. That's what you want her to do, isn't it, Sarah?"

It was easy for Aaron to see she got all the time she

needed, Courtney thought. He was no doubt hoping she'd stay in Seattle once she got there.

Sarah smiled up at Aaron, and Courtney thought she was far too forgiving. "Of course, dear," Sarah said. "And why doesn't she take Daniel along with her to help with the driving?"

"Take...Daniel?" Aaron's eyes glittered as he bent closer to Sarah. "You'd like that, wouldn't you, you she-devil. Maybe she'll fall in love with Daniel; how would that suit you?"

Sarah's face was a blank, only her eyes dancing and alive. "It never occurred to me."

Indignantly, Courtney thought it was time they stopped talking about her as if she wasn't there. She didn't care to be the subject of their coded interplay. If, indeed, it was she they were talking about. "I don't need any help driving," she said coldly. "And I'm in no danger of falling in love with anyone. Certainly not anyone at Rockhurst."

"Good for you, my dear. It's time Aaron learned that the rest of the world doesn't care to have him order their lives for them."

Aaron turned a sober face to Courtney. "I realize you're in no danger of falling in love here."

She was instantly sorry she'd been so sharp. For one thing, it wasn't good policy to talk like that to the man who was practically in charge of this house. But she was sorry, too, to have rejected so publicly the very thought of being interested in him. It had been an unkind impulse, and she didn't know what had prompted it—except that he was far too prone to try to manage everyone around him.

After a moment's thought, Aaron said, "Maybe it

would be a good thing if you'd let Daniel go along with you."

"Oh, I'll be all right," she said. Although she resented his interference, she was pleased he was concerned.

"I was thinking," he said, "that if he went with you, he could handle some business down there for us without leaving us for two days without the only transportation we can count on."

Courtney's face flamed. She had once again walked into the trap of thinking that Aaron cared what happened to her. "Of course," she said stiffly. "If Daniel wants to come along, I'll be going down early Friday morning."

"I'm sure he'll be pleased at the idea," Aaron said in his most formal manner.

AARON WAS RIGHT; Daniel had been very pleased with the plan, and he and Courtney left Rockhurst early on Friday. They had an easy drive down, and she dropped him at his hotel just after noon. They arranged that he would pick her up by cab at her apartment at six for dinner. So, with a pleasant feeling of something special to look forward to, Courtney reported in to Mr. Broberg.

The lovely jumble of the shop, the lively bustle and rumble of traffic just outside the door all filled her with a sheer joy at being back where she knew the court and the rules of the game. The quiet at Rockhurst, and the feeling that intrigue and conspiracy undermined the reality of most of what she saw, was happily absent at Broberg Galleries. Here, Courtney could believe what she heard and saw. She felt herself relaxing and expanding, as if the shell she'd been living under was being lifted.

"You are doing a good job, yes?" Mr. Broberg asked, looking at her across the cluttered desk of his little office off the sales room.

"I think so. I think you'll be pleased, really, with the collection." She explained to him the extent of Jacob's interests and described a few of the best pieces in the collection.

"And the people?" He cocked his white head at her quizzically. "You are liking the people in this mountain aerie?"

Courtney hesitated before she answered. She thought of telling Mr. Broberg about her feeling that hidden truths and veiled meanings often lay behind their conversations. Or about the secret treasure everyone hinted at or talked about. But she quickly ruled out both. There was nothing in either their coded talk or their obsession with the treasure that she couldn't handle. Besides, she was afraid Mr. Broberg would think her goal of finding the treasure was silly, or perhaps he would tell her that every family thought there was a secret cache somewhere. She didn't want his cold practicality smothering her dream of triumph. Sometimes that dream was the only thing that made Rockhurst bearable.

He hadn't asked her to gossip about the customers' personalities. He didn't want to hear about Daniel's smooth charm or Aaron's commanding presence.

"They're interesting," she said at last. "Five people, all very different. The proceeds of the sale will have to be divided between Mrs. Padgett, her grandson and her grandnephew, by the way."

"Oh? This I had not heard."

"They neglected to mention that."

"The widow Padgett neglected this, yes?"

"Well, yes, but...." She looked around the warm familiar room, where everything was as it appeared to be. The pictures, the framed licenses and diplomas hanging on the wall, the stacks of bills and receipts, the unanswered letters on the desk—everything was ordinary and usual. How could she explain Sarah's eccentricities to this good, kind, old-fashioned man? Sarah's insistence that the household goods were exclusively hers, contrary to the provisions of Jacob's will, was harmless enough, but explaining it was beyond Courtney's power. "She didn't realize we would need to be concerned with that. But I have the releases all signed."

"Ach, that is good." He put his fingertips together and studied her over their tops. "And the others? They are in favor of this sale? Or just signing off to please this old woman, Mrs. Padgett? They are helpful?"

"Yes, I guess you'd say that," she said doubtfully. "Mostly they just stay out of my way."

Mr. Broberg's big rumbling laugh filled the room. "There will be times, Courtney, my dear, when you will look back on an inventory such as this, where the family stays out of your way, and wish to be there again. To have the family stay out of your way...." He laughed again. "Ach, that is a fine thing, and rarer than blue Ming."

She smiled ruefully in agreement. She should have recognized the benefits of the Padgetts' attitude instead of grumbling about it. Her mind went back over the words, "There will be times...." He was talking about the future, further inventories, other sales. Her heart soared. He had accepted the idea of her going out to the public and was thinking forward to the future, when she would be doing such work again.

His eyes met hers and twinkled as he recognized what she was thinking. "Yes, everything seems to march well. Now." His tone changed as he prepared to get down to business. "Tell me what books you will need. What are the pieces that have puzzled you?"

The rest of the day flew by for Courtney as she tracked down the elusive information. It was only when Mr. Broberg's assistant closed the shop at five o'clock that she stowed the last book into her car and said good-night. Even the trip on the jammed freeway filled her with joy. When an irate motorist honked at her to pass, she grinned. "Hurry, hurry," she said to herself, laughing.

Before she went to her own apartment, she went upstairs to her neighbor Marie's apartment to visit Maynard. She had phoned from the gallery to say she was in town for the night, but Marie had advised her not to take Maynard home.

"It will only upset him," Marie said seriously. "He missed you terribly at first, Courtney. Prowled around meowing and scowling. But he's adjusted now, and I just think it would upset him to go home for one night. Wouldn't it, sweetums?" she said to the cat, who apparently was monitoring her phone call.

Speculating that she might have trouble regaining

custody when she came back to Seattle, Courtney was going to visit Maynard, like a parent with weekend visitation rights. At least she knew Maynard was in loving, welcoming hands. He greeted her with obvious pleasure, but typical feline reserve. While she had a cup of coffee with Marie, telling her about Rockhurst and hearing about the tenants' latest row with the stereo freak who lived next door to Courtney, Maynard rubbed her ankles. After a while he jumped onto her lap, but stayed there only a few moments, then went off by a window, where the westerly sun was warming the carpet, and cleaned his face.

"Enough is enough, right, Maynard?" Courtney said with a laugh.

Downstairs in her own apartment, she had barely enough time for a shower and a look around before Daniel came for her. His eyes flicked quickly around the room with little curiosity or interest in the few things she had bought from the gallery and proudly displayed. She was no collector, but she'd bought a few very nice prints and a pretty Chinese vase in post-revolution cloisonné. She noted with amusement that none of Jacob's passion for art objects had taken root with Daniel. His only concern at the moment was the cab waiting downstairs to take them to the Space Needle for dinner.

THEY SAT AT A WINDOW TABLE looking down as the city of Seattle seemed to revolve around them. The restaurant turned slowly and smoothly except for a slight shudder each time they came to a certain spot overlooking Queen Anne's Hill. "The starting gate,"

Daniel called it. The effect was one of standing still while the city turned. Far below them a patterned carpet of houses, trees and streets slowly gave way to hills, industrial flats and shining water. The sun was almost resting on the edge of Elliott Bay, and it laid a path of gold up to the city and washed a sheet of gold leaf over every window. A slight haze turned distant firs from dark green to a soft blue gray, but everything close sparkled brightly in the clean marine air. The restaurant continued to turn, leaving the bay behind, and soon they watched a small amphibious plane set down in Lake Union, sending up a fine feathery white plume.

"So this is your town?" Daniel asked admiringly.

Courtney looked down on the city she'd lived in and loved for nearly ten years, and was about to accept credit for its shining cleanliness, its whiter concrete, its pinker marble, its bluer water—but she hesitated. "No," she said, "it isn't. When you or Aaron stand on top of a mountain and look down, you can say, 'This is my mountain,' even though you don't own it any more than I own the city. But I can't say, 'This is my town.'"

It had suddenly occurred to her that she was not part of the city, nor the city a part of her. Although she had welcomed the noise and congestion, they were tiring her now. The confusion irritated her and sapped her strength, rather than vitalizing her.

Daniel blinked at her, and she laughed. "Never mind. I'm just...rambling on. I don't expect you to understand."

In spite of her light words, she was somehow disappointed that he didn't hear what she was saying.

Would anyone else, she wondered? Or was it that kind of nebulous drifting thought that only the thinker could appreciate? Just then the sun sank into the water, changing the light to a softer sadder shade, as if to emphasize the loneliness that washed over her unbidden, like a chill.

At the next table, the waitress was serving a young girl an enormous dessert with a fanciful name. In a bowl of smoking blue liquid was an inner bowl that held a mountain of ice cream topped with an orchid. It was the kind of dish concocted to entertain the diners for several tables around. It effectively banished Courtney's momentary depression.

The rest of the evening was a whirl of dancing, sightseeing on the wharf in the moonlight, and laughter. It was nearly closing time when they ended up in a Greek bistro in Pioneer Square and finished the night off with a feta cheese salad.

Courtney let Daniel kiss her good-night on the long cab ride back to her apartment, but she didn't let him dismiss the cab when they got there. It was one thing to go out with one of your principals, she thought, and even that is not the best idea in the world. But it would be quite another to let him come up, expecting more hospitality than she was prepared to offer. She knew that men who swore on the doorstep that all they wanted was a cup of coffee for the road were often struck by amnesia once they were inside. She didn't know what Daniel would expect, but she knew her limits fell far short of what some of the world considered acceptable today. And it would be disastrous to get into a situation where she'd have to fight Daniel off. Far better not to get into any situation at all.

ON THE WAY BACK UP THE MOUNTAIN the next day, while Courtney was taking her turn at the wheel, Daniel harangued her about being standoffish. "You're going to miss a lot of what the world has to offer, pretty lady. Some chances don't come around twice. Not that your chance with me won't. It'll come around again and again, if you want it to."

She kept her eyes on the road, as if concentrating on the curves, which were gentle this far down the mountain. Did she want her chance with Daniel to come around again? No, she realized, she didn't. Perhaps that's why it had been no big struggle to send him off to his hotel last night. Perhaps it wasn't just her high standards, or her caution about becoming involved with someone she was doing business with. Perhaps it was just that, while she liked Daniel, she didn't really want to be anything more to him than a friend. It was a relief to know exactly how she felt about at least one member of the household at Rockhurst. She turned a brilliant smile on Daniel.

"I really like you a lot, Daniel," she said. "I feel as if—please don't repeat this—as if you're the only sensible person at Rockhurst." A squirrel ran across the road in front of them, drawing her full attention back to her driving.

"Amen, Courtney."

"And I don't know when I've enjoyed being with someone more."

"Only?"

"Well, does it have to be 'only'? I mean, we like each other and we had a good time together. Isn't that enough? What's wrong with having a friend?"

She turned her head to look at him. "I don't have so many friends that I want to throw one away."

He grinned his wide engaging grin. "You're right. Why does everybody have to get to groping and grabbing right away, right?"

"You put it so delicately."

"Well, I'm sorry. But you know what I mean. I guess people get to thinking because one is a man and the other is a woman, they have to hop into bed right away."

Courtney could feel her face flaming. She sometimes thought her sheltered life in her father's studio hadn't prepared her for life in the world today.

"But it would be nice just to relax and be friends, wouldn't it?"

He laughed shortly. "Okay, okay, buddies, pals and chums it is."

Daniel was driving when they got to Harrington's store, and he pulled into the gravel driveway. "Come on, I think it's time you got to know the social life in my part of the country." He took her by the hand, and they opened a screen door to enter the tavern next to the grocery store.

Jilly's Tavern was as much a part of the life on Mt. Kulshan as the trees and the wild animals. Here was where the men sought the companionship of other men, and occasionally of the few unattached women on the mountain. It was a big, dimly lit room, with a high beamed ceiling and a row of small windows opening onto the gravel in front of Harrington's. The walls were wood planks darkened by the years; the bar stretched all along one side. Depressions were worn into the floors in front of the bar, the jukebox and the front door. A sign at the door read: ABSOLUTELY NO CAULK BOOTS, PLEASE.

A huge stone fireplace, cavernously black and empty now, filled the end wall, and a young man sat on the raised hearth, plucking wistfully at a guitar. He looked to Courtney like one of those strangely unattached young people who seemed to wander the world aimlessly, never settling long enough to disturb the dust around them.

The tall man behind the bar greeted Daniel by name, and two men, who were sitting on the black leather stools staring morosely at their beer glasses, looked up long enough to make comments about Daniel's having a pretty girl with him, and where did he find this one. Daniel waved and ignored their remarks, leading Courtney by the elbow to one of the booths under the windows. He went to the bar and brought back a glass of white wine for her and a beer for himself. The cold liquid felt good on her tongue and against her lips, and the tartness relieved her thirst. She sat sipping her wine and looked around at the funny sayings tacked up on the walls around the room, the initials carved into the booths and tables, the back bar crowded with packages of peanuts and potato chips. It seemed a much friendlier atmosphere than the slick sophisticated lounges she'd seen in Seattle.

An hour later they pulled into the yard at Rockhurst, and Aaron came storming out the door.

"Nothing's changed, I see," Daniel murmured as Aaron pulled open the door on Courtney's side.

"We were expecting you hours ago. Where have

you been? Are you all right?'' He bent over Courtney to offer his hand as she got out.

"Of course I'm all right. What could be wrong?''

"My cousin didn't. . . .''

"If you expected your cousin to be anything but a gentleman, why did you send him with me?'' She looked defiantly into the gleaming black eyes. "As it happens, you may be disappointed to hear that we had a fine time, and Daniel was, as I have always known him to be, a perfect gentleman.''

"You've only known him three weeks,'' Aaron reminded her. His eyes seemed to be twinkling with what she suspected might be amusement.

"Yes,'' she answered. "The same length of time I've known you.'' With that she turned and walked into the house.

WHEN COURTNEY CAME DOWN TO WORK the next morning, she found that her desk didn't look quite right. She couldn't put her finger on what was wrong, but she knew something was amiss. Telling herself she was being foolish, and it was just that she'd been away for two days, she sat down and started to open the locked center drawer of the little writing table.

Then she realized what had been bothering her: the lock. There were tiny scratches all around it. They were so small, they wouldn't have been noticeable to a casual observer, but Courtney, with her years of training in observation and evaluation, was not a casual observer. The infinitesimal scratches marred the fine finish of the table. She unlocked the drawer and at first saw nothing wrong. All her notebooks were there, all in what she supposed to be the right order. She hadn't made any special note of which book was on top, or which direction each faced, but they looked all right. She flipped through a couple of them, and everything seemed fine. But in the third book, she found what the intruder had been after. Or rather, she found that he or she had been after something—for one of the pages from the notebook had been torn out.

She looked carefully at the pages preceding and following the torn stub and determined that on the missing page was a list of some of the most valuable objects in Jacob's collection. Just a listing, she mused. As if someone wanted to know what the values were, what the return would be. It had happened while she was in Seattle, surely. Then she stopped and thought a moment and amended that thought. It had *probably* happened while she was in Seattle. There had been almost two days with no one working at the desk, with the huge house for people to disappear into, and with plenty of time and opportunity for anyone who wanted to pry into her work.

She sat for a long time, staring at the ragged edges of the notebook pages, trying to determine whether or not to report the break-in. To whom would she report it? Not to Sarah. She was already well aware of the possibility that someone might be trying to cheat her out of her legacy. Why upset her further? Not to Jenny, or Floyd—they were the ones who, right or wrong, would probably be blamed. And certainly not to Aaron, who would turn the whole place upside down to find out what had happened, providing he hadn't done it himself.

Could she tell Daniel? She could, but it didn't seem fair to run to him with her problems. What could he do beyond listening and sympathizing? And she would have to be careful not to call too frequently on his sympathy if she wanted him to continue to accept his role as friend-buddy-pal.

With a great effort of will, she pushed aside the fact that someone had gone through her papers, and tackled the morning's problems. But in the back of her mind, lying fretfully, was a sense of indignation and outrage, of her privacy having been violated, and she frowned as she worked.

CHAPTER SIX

IT WAS WITH DIFFICULTY that Courtney kept herself from telling Sarah about the break-in, as they had their first lunch together after Courtney's absence. But Sarah's interest in Courtney's trip and her curiosity about the evening she and Daniel had spent together got Courtney past the first troublesome impulse. She enjoyed describing the restaurant and the dancing to Sarah. It was the sort of thing she'd always envied other girls for, as she imagined them talking about their dates to their mothers. She carefully kept her feelings to herself, however, for she was sure Sarah saw the conversation more in terms of girl friends sharing confidences.

After lunch, Courtney went upstairs to get one of the books she'd brought back with her. On the second-floor landing, she stopped. Someone was moving across the hallway above her. She craned her neck to look up at the third floor, but she could see nothing.

Someone was up there. Was it someone who didn't want to be seen—because he was spying on her? Or hiding something? Or prying into the room with the icons? The icons had been listed on the missing notebook page. On impulse she tiptoed up the next flight of stairs. She wanted no confrontation. But she wanted to see, to know who was there.

A sudden flash along the floor made her jump and cry out. A small animal darted from beneath the table to a darker corner. Its tail switched, revealing a raccoon's distinctive stripes.

Courtney grasped the banister, her knees buckling with relief. She was caught between chagrin and laughter. It wasn't a cat that had startled her in the hall the day she found Sarah crying in her room. It must have been this wild creature. She went downstairs and reported the uninvited guest to Jenny, and before she had finished retelling the story to Sarah, 'he house was full of raccoon hunters.

Aaron led the way, his hands in heavy leather gloves. Daniel followed right behind him, pulling on his gloves, and Floyd was next, with a gun dangling at his side. As usual, the men were all dressed in long-sleeved shirts buttoned to the neck, in spite of the heat. They looked earnest about the whole procedure, and she began to regret having given away the animal's presence. Reluctantly, she told them where she'd seen the raccoon and was warned for the third time not to try to pick it up.

"They're nocturnal," Aaron said. "If he's out in the daytime, it means either he's sick, or he's so hungry that he's desperate."

"Either way, little one, he's no pet," Daniel told her. "So best you stay back."

Courtney remembered the raccoons she had seen at the zoo, carefully washing their food, turning it over in their hands. Those well-shaped little hands made them seem almost human. Concern for the raccoon she'd betrayed drove her up the stairs after the men.

"Floyd," Jenny screeched from the central hall,

"don't you shoot that thing off in the house. You hear?"

"Shoot?" Sarah's voice piped. "Has he got a gun?"

"Got his old .22," Jenny answered.

"Don't let him shoot it off in here," Sarah squeaked. "He'll smash something."

Aaron turned around and ordered Floyd to put the gun down.

"That critter's got rabies," Floyd said. "Else he wouldn't be out in the daytime."

Aaron leaned over the second-floor banister and shouted at Floyd, "I don't care what he's got. Put the gun down."

Floyd made a motion to put the gun on the stairs, and as soon as Aaron's back was turned, he picked it up again. Courtney let more distance develop between her and the hunters.

At the third floor, they separated. Daniel went up the east wing, on the same side as the room in which the icons were kept. Floyd turned toward the front of the house, and immediately Jenny's voice shrieked up at him. "Floyd Taylor, you stay out of my room."

Floyd ignored her, moving along quietly to the front hall. By the time Courtney got to the third floor, no one was in sight. She stood uncertainly for a moment, then, hearing a noise from the west wing, she moved cautiously into the dark hall that led to the tower. At the end of the hall a door stood open, revealing stairs that wound up along the tower wall, and from the top she could hear a shuffling, scampering noise.

Not really wanting to go up, but unable to resist, she eased herself along the wall, going up one step at a time. At the top another door opened out onto the landing, and beyond it was a small room. Except for a couple of cardboard boxes against one wall, the room was completely empty.

She turned to see if someone was behind the door, but no one was. She had heard noises up here, but the room was empty now. She looked back down the winding stairs, then turned back to the room. Aaron was standing beneath the single shuttered window.

Her thoughts tripped momentarily over the question of where Aaron had come from, then rushed on as she saw he was holding a furry and frightened raccoon. It nestled in Aaron's arms as if it had found a safe shelter, and Courtney felt so guilty at what she had done to the animal that she turned on Aaron.

"What are you going to do to that poor helpless creature now?"

Aaron blinked at her in surprise. "First I'm going to feed it, if that's okay with you."

She glared at him.

"And then I'm going to take it out to the woods. There's a fair community of raccoons over near Little Devil Falls. She'll find a family."

Courtney started down the stairs, still full of disbelief, then she stopped and turned to face him. He shut the door behind him, shooting the large bolt home. A place for a padlock hung empty, and Courtney wondered how Jenny had missed a chance to lock still another room.

Rattling the door, Aaron said, "If this was kept

closed, she couldn't have got herself into so much trouble—could you, you rascal.''

"You're...really going to let her go?''

"Of course. She's not sick. Probably just wandered in to find food and got trapped indoors. Poor thing's starving. I can feel her ribs.'' At this the raccoon turned her head and tried to bite Aaron's probing fingers. ''You ungrateful little devil.'' Laughing, he looked up from the raccoon and met Courtney's gaze.

To see laughter in his eyes shocked her. She had somehow never thought him capable of the gaiety that lit up his face now. In her confusion, she turned abruptly and started down the stairs ahead of him, her mind full of questions it would do no good to ask.

Daniel and Floyd were called in from the hunt, and Courtney stopped at the second floor. She watched as Aaron went on down to the central hall and showed his catch to Jenny and Sarah, making plans for feeding it and setting it free before dinner.

For a long time she stood leaning on the banister, staring into the emptiness that was left when Aaron had gone. He seemed to fill the house—and her thoughts—all out of proportion to his importance here. He wasn't the head of the household, and yet it seemed somehow to revolve around him without his bidding it so.

She knew she was afraid of him, and at the same time sweepingly angry with him—she couldn't speak two civil words to him. And these glimpses she kept getting—of Aaron being gentle and sweet with Sarah, and Aaron being kind to a trapped raccoon—only made her confused and all the angrier.

At last Courtney got her reference book and went to work in the library, happily spending the afternoon cataloging the jade. Jacob had attempted to segregate the pieces into dynasties and reigns, but she didn't agree with his notes on several of them. Like many collectors, his knowledge was superficial and his judgment often questionable. She hadn't even finished the preliminary listing when it was time to clean up for dinner, and she realized ruefully that she had forgotten to break for her walk. She would have to be on guard against that in the future.

As she changed for dinner, she thought of the raccoon, out by now in her own environment where Aaron had taken her, having dinner with her friends. As if it had been skirting the question all day, touching and backing off like a dragonfly at a milkweed, her mind settled lightly on the riddle of where Aaron had come from when he had appeared so suddenly in the tower room. In her mind's eye she saw the tiny half-circular room—empty. She replayed the steps of looking behind the door, peering down the stairs, and seeing no one. Then, without a sound, there had been Aaron, holding the raccoon. The only answer that fit was a secret panel.

Her common sense balked at the thought. It was so...theatrical. And yet, hadn't Jacob Padgett been beyond the ordinary in many things? His treatment of his daughter, Anabelle, when she returned home, his obsessive collecting—most of all, his insistence that there was a hidden treasure—were all melodramatic. A man living in this fantastic house, given to excesses himself—such a man might very well have a concealed door in a remote tower.

And if he did, she thought, that's surely where he would hide his secret treasure.

As she brushed her hair, she worried over asking the family about the tower and the room. They must have looked there for Jacob's hoard; they all admitted they'd been searching. Leaning over the dresser top to put on fresh lipstick, she stopped and stared unseeing into the smoky mirror. Perhaps the others hadn't recognized the treasure when they saw it. Or...perhaps they didn't know about the secret door and what lay beyond it.

But Aaron knew.

She straightened up, resolved not to mention the tower while Aaron was near. He had brought the raccoon from beyond some shrouded passageway, she was convinced. Once she'd accepted the possibility of a secret panel, she was a little surprised at how easily its existence became established in her mind.

Had Aaron already found Jacob's mysterious riches? Was that why he alone in the family spoke as if he was sure there was no treasure? Was he trying to lead everyone off the scent? If Jenny's suspicions were correct that one of the Boys was trying to cheat Sarah, then Aaron might be hiding his gleanings there in the tower until he could safely claim them... until he could steal them from Sarah.

COURTNEY WENT DOWN the long, curving staircase to dinner, thinking that it wasn't the value of what he might steal, or the criminality that struck her; it was simply the injustice of it. That this injustice could lead to something more serious if it were uncovered—or even threatened with discovery—didn't enter her thoughts for more than an instant. In her world violence was the misuse of clashing colors, or a scene depicted on canvas.

After dinner the family more or less settled in the parlor, except for Aaron, who left grumbling about checking on Floyd while it was still light out. Courtney wondered what Samantha would think if she knew her slinky red sports car was playing second fiddle to a pickup that wasn't even running. Behind the house Floyd had the pickup torn down into a jumble of parts that didn't look as if they'd ever be a truck again. When Courtney had turned down Daniel's invitation to play gin, take a walk, dance, or go to Jilly's, all with equal firmness, he gave up with a shrug and a grin. Before Sarah could notice, he too was gone.

Leaving Sarah and Jenny, who were deeply engrossed in speculation about when Winston was going to announce his annual party, Courtney said good-night and hurried upstairs. At the second-floor landing, she stopped and listened. Satisfied that no one had followed her, she went up to the third floor and on to the tower steps. She had no intention of going up there at night. She had a fleeting picture of one of those stupid story heroines in a filmy nightgown, carrying a kerosene lamp into the castle dungeon. But this was very different. It was still daylight, she was wearing her yellow dress, and this wasn't a castle.

Besides, there wasn't anything strange or eerie about the tower. It was merely isolated and deserted, but certainly not haunted or cursed. Still, she was determined to go up quickly before the short mountain twilight was swallowed up in the shadows of the somber trees. Now was the time, while there was still light coming through the little west-facing window.

The tower was bolted, as Aaron had left it, and the padlock hasp hung empty. She opened the door and went into the small room where Aaron had appeared with the raccoon in his arms. Now that she was able to take a better look, she saw that the room was too small to fill the tower top. The westerly light from the sun was streaking through the shutters of the only window. Three walls were plastered and painted a dingy tan, and the fourth wall was paneled in a pattern of rectangles that might have come from the Jacobean library of a gentlemen's club.

Looking closer, with almost a twinge of disappointment, she saw that there was no secret panel after all. No attempt had been made to hide the recess in the wall. One row of panels, from ceiling to floor, was depressed just enough to slip behind the others like a sliding closet door. With a slight push, it slid silently to the left, revealing another room, smaller and darker than the first. It had no windows or skylight, and the only light came from the outer room where she stood.

Like an old-fashioned attic, the room was stuffed with the discards of generations. A dress form puffed its bosom out beside a wicker baby buggy and an inevitable broken rocker with its well-indented cushions still tied to the seat. The layer of dust covering the trunks and boxes had been disturbed, thick here, patchy and streaked there. The odor reminded Courtney that the raccoon had nested in there for at least a week.

But on the small square table that tilted toward its broken leg stood a kerosene lamp, with a flat circular reflector, newly polished, and fresh oil in its well. She saw then that the sealing tape on the cardboard cartons had been torn and many of them stood with their flaps hanging loose. Someone had been going through everything, no doubt looking for Jacob's treasure.

But that was what she had expected. The point was, had he found it? Quickly she began opening cartons, rummaging through the first couple of layers and slamming their flaps back as she eliminated collections of well-used toys, out-of-date clothes, and broken appliances. The two trunks held more clothes, baby blankets and sweaters, heavy worsted overcoats. In the close gloom, she opened carton after carton.

Her back was beginning to protest by the time she had taken a quick look at every box and container in the room. Then she remembered that there were a couple of cartons in the outer room. The light out there, shutter-striped and orange with the fading sky, was strong enough to show up the layer of dust that had settled on her dress. Why hadn't she thought to change back to her jeans instead of racing up so impatiently. All those lectures she'd had on being impetuous and leaping before she'd thought things through hadn't seemed to do much good, she realized.

With this depressing thought in mind, she began to open the cartons that were lined up against the wall of the outer room. She groaned as she saw that the first was full of old books. Not Morroco-bound, gold-stamped or in any way special. Just old books. Galsworthy. Hardy. Eliot. She picked up *The Mill on the Floss*, noting in a professional way that its condition was good, the spine firm, the bindings solid. She supposed these had been taken from the library downstairs to make room for the jade cabinet and the new shelves of porcelain. Taking up a grayed copy of *The Travelers' London*, full of dreary photographs of Edwardians on desolate city streets, she became aware that she was being very careful not to make a sound. Her mind had begun to tiptoe. She laid the book down without a sound.

She stood absolutely still, hardly breathing. The silence closed in. Some breath, some tiny stirring in the air made her turn around. The door was closing. Slowly, quietly. She started toward it and it slammed shut...as if it had seen her coming...as if someone were watching.

The hair at the back of her neck tingled. She clutched the doorknob, and it turned loosely in her hand. She grasped it with both hands, trying to fit it into the groove, but nothing took hold.

Discouraged, she stopped and stared at the door. In the silence, she heard a small noise—hardly more than a scratching: the tiny rasping sound of metal being slowly, surreptitiously drawn across metal. Instinctively she put her hand out to the door, and suddenly felt it now fit more solidly into the jamb. The bolt had been thrown.

She knew she should scream. She should call out, pound on the door, do anything to make a noise, sound an alarm. But she was frozen. Unable to believe what had happened, she couldn't react. She waited, listening. Pressing her ear against the heavy wooden door, she heard her own pulses throbbing. At last her mind accepted the unacceptable—someone had locked her in there. Anger hit her then, and she was able to move. Banging her fists on the door, she cried out at the top of her lungs. But she soon gave that up. Something about the quality of her voice told her the room was practically soundproof.

When that thought had sunk in, she stood for a long moment, propped against the door. She wasn't thinking now of getting out or not getting out, of escaping or being trapped. Her mind was blank, afraid to look ahead This instant, the present, was all she could handle. She clenched her fists and fought down panic.

At last the unreasoning fear receded and she could think again. Her jaw ached and she realized that she had dug her nails into the palms of her hands—little red half-moons stood in a row like sentinels of fear. She faced the incredible, impossible thing that had happened. She had no idea why she had been locked into the tower, and no time to wonder about it. All she wanted was to find a way out. She stood looking around her prison. Perhaps the other room....

But there was no exit in the smaller room. It was only a partitioned-off part of the tower top, with no door or window of its own. Just to be sure, she walked along the sides, feeling the crumbling walls for a door. There was nothing. But there was something wrong in the room, and she couldn't think what it was. She stood peering through the gloom, trying to see what was bothering her. Then she knew. The room smelled different than it had only a few moments ago. The rank raccoon odor was overlaid with another smell. There was gas coming in.

At first she denied the possibility. Jenny had said the pipes were cut off long ago. Or had she said that, Courtney wondered. Had she only said that there used to be gas all over the house? And that the electric wiring stopped before the third floor had been wired? She couldn't remember exactly what Jenny had said. But it was clear that there was gas in the room now. Rousing herself, she searched the room, unable to find the source.

It wasn't until she had been all around the walls again that she realized she should get out of that tiny, windowless enclosure before the fumes got too strong. Another wave of panic swept over her. She ran into the outer room and rammed the sliding panel closed. She threw herself at the hall door, desperately trying to force it open, banging and screaming when it held tightly.

Even as she cried out, she knew it was useless. The house was built so solidly that sounds hardly carried from room to room, let alone from floor to floor. And everyone was down in the parlor. No, she remembered, Daniel had gone out. And Aaron was out helping Floyd with the pickup. Her mind skittered past the thought that perhaps everyone only thought he was out there.

She went to the window, but it was too high for a good view. Shutters on the inside of the window blocked the way. She tugged at one of the book cartons and pushed it into place under the window. The second box was too heavy to lift. She stood up, panting, and realized the gas odor was beginning to seep into the outer room. Out of fear, she found the strength to lift the box onto the first one.

Her head was inches from the low, sloping ceiling when she climbed up on the two boxes, and the air was hotter. She still couldn't get at the window to break the glass. The rusted latch of the shutters wouldn't give as she banged at it. On tiptoes she peered over the top of the shutters, squinting against the lowering sun. She could see the yard, the shed, Jenny's vegetable garden. Even the corner of the porte cochere with the Paul's scarlet rose swinging in the evening breeze was visible. As she watched, Floyd ambled out from the barn and over to the pickup, pulling an oily red rag from his pocket and wiping his hands. Even from the height of the tower, she could see his look of concentration as he bent over the engine. But where was Aaron, she wondered?

She banged on the shutter latch with her fist, then with the heel of her shoe. The latch was rusted solid. She pushed the center rod that joined the slats, moving the louvers like a signal. But the movement was too slight to be seen three floors down, she knew. She looked around for some means of catching Floyd's eye. She had no scarf, no handkerchief to wave. She shaded her eyes as the sun moved away from a tall tree and hit the window, unfiltered by the branches. The sun, streaming onto the window, was her only hope. Remembering the shiny lamp reflector in the other room, she scrambled down from the boxes, cursing herself for being so slow to put together the sun and the louvered shutters and the need to signal. Now she would have to hurry to make use of the sun while it lasted and pray that Floyd would see her signal in time.

Facing the sliding panel to the small inner room, she hesitated. To open it would allow more of the foul-smelling gas to escape into the outer room. But there was no way of avoiding it. Holding her breath, she pushed the panel open and dashed inside to grab the lamp and scurry out again. Jamming the panel back in place, she let her breath out. Spots danced before her eyes against a reddish background that faded and turned green.

Spilling oil in her haste, she got the chimney off the lamp and bent the reflector back so she could get it as close to the window as possible. Climbing back onto the boxes, she held the reflector up against the shutters. The blood pounded in her temples as she examined the lamp to see if it was truly catching the sun's rays.

Moving the louvers up and down, she frantically tried to remember some Morse code. All she could think of was *dit dit dit da*. But what was the signal for SOS? May Day. May Day.

Suddenly it came to her. *Dit dit dit da da da*. Over and over. It didn't matter which was S and which was O. Keeping her eye on the angle of the reflector to make sure it caught the light, she snatched brief glimpses over the top of the shutter at Floyd.

But nothing, it seemed, could draw Floyd's attention from the puzzle of the pickup's engine. The sun slid momentarily behind the tops of some tall firs on the peak of Mt. Kulshan, and she felt the chill through her whole being. If Floyd didn't look up soon, the sun would be gone. She willed him to look her way, but her thoughts weren't strong enough. Nothing was going to work, she thought, slumping against the shutters.

Then a movement of Floyd's head alerted her. He looked up but not as far as the tower, only toward the back door of the house. Jenny marched down the back steps and across the yard to the truck. From her posture, Courtney guessed that Jenny was scolding him. With one hand on her hip, she shook a finger in Floyd's face and then pointed toward the house. She bent close, and Floyd tucked his head between his shoulders as if to escape. Finally he straightened, and again Jenny pointed to the house. Courtney thought she must be ordering him to get in and do whatever it was he was supposed to have done.

Jenny was pointing to the upper stories, and at last Floyd looked up. As he did, Courtney jerked the louvers frantically. *Dit dit dit da da da*. She could just make out his puzzled frown. But he could be frowning at Jenny's bossing. With her arm aching from working the louvers, Courtney kept watch on the yard below. Floyd returned to the pickup, but now Aaron was standing there beside him. Aaron looked toward the house, toward the tower. He said something to Floyd, and Floyd gestured toward the truck.

Was Aaron purposely distracting Floyd's attention away from the house? With another quick glance at the tower, Aaron crossed the yard, and in a moment Floyd threw down his rag and followed him.

Courtney climbed down from the boxes and stumbled across to the door, pressing her ear against it. An eternity passed as she waited to know whether or not Aaron was coming to the tower. Had he seen her signal? Had he understood it? Or... if it was Aaron who locked the door, would he ignore her desperate plea?

It was painful to think that Aaron had locked her in the tower. Still, the idea stuck in her mind. He could have seen her going up to the third floor and followed her. Perhaps she had inadvertently found Jacob's treasure—found it and failed to recognize it, as others at Rockhurst probably had.

She held her head in both hands. Her thought processes were muddled. She was trying to find a motive for Aaron, and at the same time she didn't want to believe he had been the one to lock the door. But it was hard to think through the buzzing in her head, which had started with the sound of one bee and had grown to that of an angry swarm.

But if she had seen the treasure and failed to recognize it, who would believe that? She was the art expert, after all. If Aaron knew she had seen it, whatever it was, he would think she knew its worth. He knew where she'd been working, just as he knew everything else that went on at Rockhurst. He would know, too, where the supposedly dead gas lines were.

She shook her head irritably. She had been over the whole thing before, surely. Her theory would fit anyone and everyone. Wearily, she slumped to the floor, leaning against the door. She was tired and drowsy, she realized; it was no wonder she couldn't think straight. The buzzing in her head was making her feel exhausted. It was hopeless, anyhow, waiting for someone who wasn't coming. She rested her head against the door.

It seemed a long time later when a sound aroused her and she snapped her head up. There was someone on the stairs. She closed her eyes in relief and listened to the steady thump of feet. The noise in her head was deafening now, but she struggled to grasp a thought that kept intruding. Hadn't she just been thinking that Aaron was the cause of her being here? If that was true, he could be coming now to finish the job, to be certain the gas had worked. Sudden fear flooded out her joy at being rescued.

Struggling to her feet and hanging onto the doorjamb, she listened as he fumbled with growing irritation, shaking the door and hitting the latch, trying to get the bolt free. With every second, every angry growl from the other side of the door, her fear grew. When at last the knob turned and the door swung open, Courtney saw his face, livid with fury, his eyes blazing. She made a rush to avoid his restraining hands and flee to safety. Instead, the room spun, the ceiling tilted with a lurching swoop, and she collapsed into Aaron's waiting arms. He lifted her free of the floor and started down the stairs. Her last conscious thought was that he was carrying her off and she didn't know where.

CHAPTER SEVEN

COURTNEY FELT HERSELF being carried, put down, fussed with. Someone chafed her wrists roughly. Gentler hands pushed the hair off her forehead. Voices began to drift toward her, and the green veil of unconsciousness thinned.

"...back in that hospital."

But she wasn't in a hospital; she was at Rockhurst. She could see the familiar skylight, the paneled walls.

"...going back to that place with all them crazy people."

Who was that? She scowled over the puzzle.

"No one's going back to the sanatorium." That was Aaron's voice. She smiled at solving part of the mystery. "Just get that out of your head. No doctors, no sanatorium." Aaron's voice changed, softened. "Well, look who's back with us. Feeling better? You're not sick, are you?"

She wished he hadn't mentioned that. She thought she might be, but she shook her head and tried to get up. Aaron helped her to her feet, telling her to take it easy. Her breath began to come more easily, and although her head pounded with a savage pain, she began to think more clearly. She had been locked in the tower, with the gas turned on. She remembered thinking about Aaron...that he had done it. And now he had changed his mind. She drew away from his supporting arms. She pulled back and stumbled against Floyd, who was standing on her other side She fought to get hold of her emotions. Aaron mustn't see how frightened she was. He would use her weakness against her.

But Aaron had seen the fear in her widened eyes, her jerky movements. "You're all right now. You're safe," he said. "Floyd, get in there and see about that gas. I think the valve's in. . . ."

"I know where it is." Floyd lumbered off.

Courtney was left alone to face Aaron. She forced herself to look up at him. "Why did you do that?"

They had seen her signal and come to see what it was all about, he said. They hadn't thought of it as a distress sign, but merely a summons, and they had come to investigate. They hadn't known they were coming up to save her.

"You know what I mean." Her voice was hardly more than a whisper. "Why did you lock me in there?"

"Lock. . . . You can't mean that!" Aaron's voice had dropped to meet hers. "You think I tried to kill you?"

Suddenly she remembered the words she'd heard as she was coming to. Doctors and sanatoriums. Going back. Was he insane? She felt her heart lurch, and the pain was unbearable. She staggered. When she looked up again at Aaron's face, she saw an echoing pain there. Then his face went blank and impassive with such a practiced ease that she thought, *This is the mask he hides behind*. But she was too groggy to hold onto the thought. There was nothing to give him away except a lingering sadness in his eyes.

"I see." His fists were at his sides, the knuckles white. "There isn't much I can do about how you feel, or what you choose to believe. Except to assure you you're wrong."

She turned her head and didn't see the look of loss and anguish that crossed his face.

At that moment Floyd came back, saying the valve had been pushed open. "Probably got knocked open when I put them cartons of stuff away that Miss Courtney said was finished and ready to be shipped out."

Courtney knew that didn't explain why she had not smelled gas when she first entered the room, but she kept her thoughts to herself.

Aaron advised her to sit down and she obeyed, seating herself on the stairs. "Miss Courtney thinks someone locked her in the tower on purpose," Aaron told Floyd.

Floyd guffawed, as if it might have been a practical joke. "That's dumb. Who'd do a dumb thing like that?"

"I don't know," Courtney said, keeping her eyes on the carpet. It hurt to move her head, and she didn't want to look at Aaron. "But someone locked the door and tried to kill me, or frighten me badly."

Suddenly Floyd sobered up. "Are you serious? Look, I know you're all shook up and all, but that ain't right." Suddenly he began to sweat, and his hands trembled. "You shouldn't ought to say things like that."

"It's all right, Floyd," Aaron said. "She thinks it was me."

Floyd watched him from the corners of his eyes. Distrust was evident in his face, as if he suspected a trap.

"The door at the top of the tower stairs hangs on a slant," Aaron began tonelessly. "I think it drifted shut. The same as it did on the raccoon."

" 'Course it did," Floyd agreed. "Old house, settling and all. Geez, there ain't a level floor or a door that's hung proper in the whole place."

"But the bolt?" She addressed herself to Floyd. "Didn't you see that it was locked?"

"Slant does that," he answered. "Door fell shut and the jolt thrown the bolt. I oughta know. I got to fix stuck doors and loose doors all the time around here."

It all sounded logical enough, she thought. And her own jiggling of the doorknob could have shifted the bolt. Not that she believed it for a moment. But in the face of reasonable explanations, it would sound foolish, even hysterical, to cry murder. She decided to keep her fears to herself until her head was clearer and she was able to think without the dizziness that ebbed, then rose again to engulf her.

"This isn't the time to look for an answer," Aaron said. "You should be resting." Without another word he scooped her up from the stairs where she was sitting. Too confused and weak to resist, she lay in his arms as he carried her to her room.

When he had put her down on the big four-poster and pulled the comforter up around her, he stood looking at her impassively for a moment, then left.

She lay with her eyes closed, half-asleep, her head still throbbing, unable to put the experience out of her mind. She was again in the tower, hearing Aaron's footsteps come up the stairs, one at a time. But he opened the door with ease and came nearer. He carried a fancy-dress mask on a stick and held it in front of his face as he came to the bed where she lay watching him. Dropping the mask, he came nearer still and leaned over her. She saw he was dressed all in white, like a patient in a hospital. She cried out and he drifted away until he was across the room. Then she saw he was wearing a strait-jacket and his arms were pinned behind him. It was cruelly tight. She stretched out her arms, offering to help him, and he came closer again. She felt warm and tender, and she reached out to him. He put a hand gently on her forehead. Perhaps he kissed her. She smiled and sighed sensuously as he leaned closer and she lifted her face to meet his. But his face was dark and scowling, blazing with anger as he shouted at her. Her own scream woke her up.

She lay there trembling for some time. Who was this man Aaron? Was he an ogre, who touched her gently? Or was he a gallant knight who turned into a monster? Her dream had been just like her real relationship with him. She couldn't tell the man from the beast. And suddenly she had the strange feeling that the dream hadn't been all dream. He had been in the room. To check on her, perhaps, and see that she was all right. And the gentle touch on her forehead had not been imagined, but real. He had kissed her in her sleep.

No, that was silly, a schoolgirl's rapturous fancy. And yet it had seemed so real. But then, she thought, that's what fantasy was all about. Impossible dreams that seemed real.

Wide awake now, she lay staring at the embossed ceiling until long after she heard Sarah being helped to her room. Unbelievably, in the face of what had happened, it was still only a little after nine when Courtney decided she couldn't lie still another second. She put on a robe and slippers and, looking cautiously up and down the hallway first, went to Sarah's room.

As usual, Sarah's door stood open and the yellow light of a lamp poured out, drowning the last of the dusk filtering through the skylight. Courtney stopped a moment to compose her thoughts and pull herself together. She couldn't just burst in on Sarah, accusing Aaron of attempted murder. Quickly she went over in her mind what she wanted to say. She ruled out any mention of the tower. Sarah mustn't get the idea she was a silly hysterical girl. Besides, now that her head had cleared and she had thought about the explanations Floyd and Aaron had given, she had just enough doubt about the incident to be hesitant to talk about it.

As she stood silently, gathering her thoughts, she heard a familiar sound. It was Sarah's soft sobbing. Hesitantly, she took two steps toward Sarah's door. It was the second time she had interrupted a very private moment. Still, if she could help.... At the door, she stopped again. Sarah was sitting up in bed, propped all around with pillows and wrapped in angora. On her lap a black leather document case lay open, its contents strewn across Sarah's knees. She was holding a folded yellowing paper in one hand, and dabbing a handkerchief to her eyes with the other.

For an instant Courtney wondered, with a twinge of resentment, how Sarah could be so engrossed in her private affairs when she, Courtney, had just had such a narrow escape. But of course, Sarah knew nothing about it, she realized. It was like waking from a nightmare to find the world going about its business; it seems incredible that no one knows of the terror you've dreamed.

A suppressed sob from Sarah brought her back to reality, and she silently backed away. She couldn't force herself and her problems on Sarah again.

In the end, she decided not to mention the incident to anyone. Aaron, however, apparently did, for Jenny grumbled the next day about Aaron wasting time changing the door to the tower and putting it on a spring so it would stay open unless someone closed it on purpose.

"Says you got yourself locked in there." Jenny peered at her.

Aaron was putting on a fine show of concern, Courtney thought. The head of the household taking care of the chores, and reaffirming the accidental nature of the incident. She had to admit it was what he might do if he were innocent. But it was also what he would surely do if he were guilty.

She soon found that, in spite of her own resolve not to talk about what happened, everyone already knew. Sarah fussed and Jenny complained, and Floyd said even Daniel had asked him about it. Courtney had slipped out the back door, grateful for the fresh air, when the time came for her afternoon break. Seeing Floyd at work again on the pickup, she had gone to talk to him. She was pleased that Daniel had shown an interest but, somehow, not stirred. How was it that the very mention of Aaron's name could raise such a storm of feelings in her—all of them negative, she hastened to remind herself—and the thought of Daniel only made her smile briefly? Daniel was sweet and charming and considerate, and he had shown that with a little encouragement he would be all that and more. But she wasn't inclined to give him any sign that she welcomed his attention. She leaned against the fender of the truck wondering if she was making another mistake. Perhaps...

"I told him I only know what Aaron said," Floyd grumbled. " 'Look,' he says, 'there's someone up there.' So naturally, up we go. When Aaron says, everybody jumps."

Again she was filled with the churning feelings that any discussion of Aaron caused. She put both elbows on the fender and bent her head closer to Floyd's. He was reaching under the hood for a wire, his attention on the truck.

"Why does everyone jump when Aaron speaks?" she asked.

"I don't know. Because he's the only one with any sense. 'Cause he's the boss." Floyd looked up from his work to glare at her. "Because I have to jump when anyone speaks. I take orders from him, and Jenny and Sarah, and everybody around here. It's Floyd this, and Floyd that. I got half a notion to dump this job and just take off. You got no idea how bad it gets around here."

"Why do you stay, then? Why not leave?"

"I will, by golly." He stared at her as if she had just told him something amazing. "I'll go to my cousin's, over at Walla Walla. I'll be glad to get shed of this place." He started to turn away from the truck and stopped. His shoulders slumped and his chin fell. "I ain't even got the bus fare to Walla Walla."

He didn't seem to know when he was due to get paid, and Courtney wondered if Aaron put off the payroll so often that Floyd couldn't keep track. No wonder he had no money. "The bus fare would be an awful lot of money," Floyd said. "I don't know. Twelve, fifteen dollars, maybe." He draped himself over the cab door. "What's the difference? I'll never get away from here."

"You sound as if you're a slave."

"I don't know what else you'd call it. At everybody's beck and call. Never enough money to go anywheres. Always being threatened with...." He broke off.

"Threatened with what?"

"Nothing, it don't matter." He looked quickly around the yard, as if afraid he'd been overheard. He licked his lips and rubbed his hands down the sides of his pants. "It don't matter, I tell you."

She had no idea what had suddenly upset him so, but she knew it was wrong for anyone to be so afraid. Impulsively, she offered to lend him the bus fare to get to his cousin's and promised to see that Aaron mailed him his back wages. He stared open-mouthed as she made her offer and nodded his acceptance. She went upstairs, grateful for the sound-swallowing effect of the high ceilings and carpets. In a few moments she was back in the yard and found Floyd still standing where she had left him. She handed him two twenty-dollar bills. It was all she had with her.

"When will you leave?" she asked.

"I don't know. Got to find the right time. When he's busy or away. Soon's he finds out, he'll come lookin' for me."

"He's not going to chase you, Floyd." Surely his fears were exaggerated.

"You don't think so? You wait and see." A crafty look came into his eyes. "I ain't telling anyone when I'm leaving. That way you won't be able to tell him." He crumpled the bills and stuffed them into his pants pocket. With a quick sideways glance at her, he stomped away toward the barn.

She stood and watched him disappear into the cavernous barn and suddenly wondered if she'd done the right thing. His fears seemed so unreasonable. . . . But surely that was the very reason what she did was right. Of course it was. She squared her shoulders, turned away from the barn and marched out of the yard. Now let's see Aaron frighten Floyd into staying, she thought.

She took one of the many paths leading up the hill into the woods, hardly noticing which way she was going. Her mind, carefully directed away from what Aaron would say and do when he found out Floyd had left, was on the two big pieces of news at Rockhurst. The first was a forest fire in the national forest to the east. In Seattle they heard about the fires each year, but it was as if they were occurring on some distant planet. It was interesting here on Mt. Kulshan to hear Aaron and Daniel discussing the progress of what she had come to think of as "our fire." Their comments, as the fire passed Ridgeback Summit and then jumped Silver Creek, reminded her of the way she would talk about avoiding rush-hour traffic on Aurora Boulevard.

The other news certainly more interesting and exciting to most of the household, was of Winston Coe's annual party, where the city folk got to meet the country folk, and vice versa. Ever since the invitations arrived in the morning's mail—one for Sarah, one for each of the Boys, and one for Courtney—Sarah had been in a state of kittenish delight. The party had distracted her from worrying about what had happened to Courtney in the tower and had displaced old movies as Sarah's favorite topic of conversation.

Courtney's mind was so filled with the talk and preparations for Winston's party that she was barely watching where she was going, except to note vaguely that she hadn't been this way before. Then the path she was following took a sharp turn, and a meadow opened up at her feet. The salal and huckleberry and the bracken fern hung around the edges of the clearing and peered over a dilapidated wrought-iron fence like urchins on the outside of a party. The knee-high fence surrounded a square area about the size of a city block. Remnants of a gate leaned away from the tall golden rye and foxtails of the field, and flakes of rust and black paint came off on Courtney's fingers. A large piece of the fence was missing at one side.

The smell of dry grass rose up from the green and gold floor, and there was a soft, insistent humming of insects. In the distance a squirrel clicked out a message, and a lone raven punctuated the quiet air with a sharp caw. At first all Courtney saw in the clearing was a vine-covered stump and the golden grass. Then, near the foot of the stump, she saw the grave marker half-hidden in the high weeds.

As she started to cross the little field toward it, she began to notice other low gray stones, as if they were sprouting up all around. The very old ones at the back, standing not quite straight, were thin gray white slabs with arched tops and barely visible inscriptions. Near the center, several small, round-topped stones huddled together, and nearby were two larger ones. At the far left was a new stone, thicker, with less grass covering the still-mounded earth. She circled the others and read the inscription, clear and precise in the pinkish marble:

Jacob Elia Padgett
1888-1976

Well, it was to the point, she thought. No nonsense about it. She wandered toward the cluster of small graves. The stones here, barely readable, all reflected similar stories of babies born into a too harsh world, as if "Infant Padgett" was often not here long enough to acquire a name.

The larger twin stones, for "Mathilda, Wife and Mother" and "Josephus Padgett," carried grotesque death's heads at the top, bare skulls intended, she supposed, to remind one of the transitory quality of life and the flesh. She shivered in the oppressive heat.

If Jacob had had brothers and sisters other than the infants, they were not represented among the crumbling stones here. To the side, halfway up the square, was a small, plain marker that read:

> Charity Padgett
> second wife of
> Josephus Padgett
> Died 1920

Apparently, no one had cared enough to find out when she was born.

Courtney continued around and came to another set of stones that told of a succession of childbirths and early deaths. One, with three names, read:

> Carried off by Influenza
> Jan. 1922

The mother's stone read:

> Elizabeth Padgett
> Née Watson
> Born 1900   Died 1928

That would be Jacob's first wife, she thought. And poor Sarah, would she have a stone reading, "Jacob Padgett's second wife?"

As she wandered through the slippery dry grass she came across one more grave. Off in a corner a flat marker was sunk into the ground. She wouldn't have seen it at all except that a pot of chrysanthemums was placed at its head. The flowers were wilted with thirst, the lower leaves yellowing and the petals limp and drooping. It seemed to her a shame not to rescue them, whomever they belonged to, and she looked around for water. There would be no water piped up this far from the house, but there was an enamelware saucepan lying beside the isolated grave, apparently used to fetch water from the stream she could hear nearby.

Picking up the pot and following the sound of the water, she edged through a gap in the fence at the back of the meadow. She found the trail and, about a hundred feet farther along, the stream.

When she had carried the water back and poured it carefully onto the plant and into the soil, she took time to read the marker:

Anabelle Padgett
1928-1953

Most of the members of this family certainly died young, she thought, still kneeling beside the grave. She remembered now what Jenny had said—that Jacob's daughter Anabelle had run away. And that Jacob had been very angry with her when she came back. And someone—she couldn't recall who—had called Aaron a bastard. Perhaps it wasn't just a figure of speech. She looked at the dates again. Aaron must have been born shortly after World War II; if he was a 'love child,'' Anabelle didn't get to love him for very long.

She poured the last few drops of water over the leaves and stood up. All alone in that deserted graveyard, in the unrelenting sun, she stepped back, and her shoulder touched something warm and solid. She screamed and dropped the pan. She tried to bolt, but a pair of strong arms restrained her. Or supported her?

"Here, here, dear girl." Winston Coe's light voice reached through her fright. "I'm not going to hurt you."

Her laugh was sharp in the still air, brittle with relief. "It's you," she said, trying to catch her breath. "I'm so glad it's you."

"Who were you expecting, my dear? Hamlet's father's ghost?"

"No, not exactly " She leaned against his strength.

"Anabelle's father's ghost, perhaps." He took her by the shoulders, and she straightened up and managed a weak smile

"Maybe. I don't know." Pulling herself together, she looked at him sheepishly. "I just...you startled me."

"Apparently." He raised an eyebrow. "And you couldn't have looked guiltier."

"You knew her—Anabelle—didn't you?"

"Knew her? Oh, yes." He looked at the faded flowers on the grave. "You see...they put flowers on her grave, then neglect to water them. All her life I watched them do things like this. Make a show of doing what's right, then...." With the toe of a slim shoe that seemed miraculously dust-free and shiny even here, he tapped the flower pot lightly, shaking a few dead leaves from the stems.

"And all the while," he went on, "I could see it happening, and I stood by, absolutely helpless." With a sad smile, he sighed. Then as if he sensed that his performance was just a shade too brave and wistful, he turned to her and said brightly, "But that's all in the past now, isn't it?"

"I don't know," she answered. "In this place I don't know if anything is really in the past. The past won't...won't stay in its place."

"Doesn't do to let oneself become fanciful."

"I just mean that everyone is so bound by memories and old grudges that no one acts just on what's happening today."

"My dear child, you don't think that's an exclusive characteristic of Rockhurst, surely?"

She smiled at him and shrugged. He was right, of course, and she thought she should have been the first one to see it. Her own life was being directed by the debts her father had left, and then soon afterward Ken's desertion. Even her reaction to Winston, that slight edge of disbelief, was because of her father and because of Ken. Men seemed able to pretend so well. But maybe Winston wasn't pretending. "You were fond of her," she said, thinking of Anabelle.

"A poor pale word. I wanted to marry her. Quite desperately wanted to marry her. I offered her what little I could." He spread his hands. "It wasn't... wasn't what she wanted."

She knew he didn't mean he had offered her material things. It was strange how little thought people who have plenty of money give to its importance. It was something else he couldn't offer Anabelle that was missing. But she sensed he wasn't going to tell her any more.

"Well," he said, straightening his sloped shoulders and tugging at the cuffs of his jacket. "Mustn't waste the day dreaming of what might have been, must we? I was just on my way over to Rockhurst to remind one and all of my party Saturday night and to apologize for the invitations arriving rather late." He explained that the date had depended on when his city friends were free to come up to the mountains. "Samantha, of course, will be back." His eyebrows seemed to be signaling something to her, but she refused to consider what roguish meaning they intended.

Nonetheless, her mind had been caught by the information; she hadn't known that Samantha had left the neighborhood. She supposed that absence accounted for Aaron's being in the yard working on the pickup last night. She brushed the thought aside with irritation. What did she care where Samantha was, or what effect her presence or absence had on Aaron?

Winston was complaining about the long walk to Rockhurst. "But I refuse to dignify this ridiculous arrangement they call a party line by using it unless absolutely forced to do so. Better to trudge through this abominable heat." He looked heavenward. "Will it never rain?"

She laughed. The heat hadn't displaced one hair on Winston's head, or caused the slightest wrinkle in his expensively tailored denims. Even the slender silk scarf tied at his neck looked crisp and fresh. "No need to remind us of your party," she said, wondering if she need commit herself to attending. She was unsure of her social standing with the Padgetts—she was hired help, after all. It was silly to still be discomfited by Samantha's barbed remark so long ago, but the bitchiness of the comment was in its truth. Besides, she knew too well the course of large cocktail parties with artsy people. Those faculty parties with her father.... Still, she liked Winston in spite of her reservations and thought perhaps his party would somehow be different. She hurried on, saying, "Your party is all Sarah has talked about today. I think she's tried on every dress she owns at least twice."

"Yes, well, she'll wear the cranberry crepe."

"How do you know?"

"She always does. Sets off her hair. It will be an added glory for her to have you along under her wing, so to speak. You are coming?" Without waiting for an answer, he turned and started toward the gate, with a movement that was half salute, half bow. "Sarah likes to have the invitation reinforced with a personal reminder. But if you'll deliver my message—that they're expected, eightish—I won't bother to slog through the heat."

Thinking that whatever Winston Coe did, it could never be conceived of as "slogging," she said, "Sarah will be disappointed that she missed seeing you."

"Yes, well, we know she won't take offense four days before the party, don't we? Ta." He turned and went down the slope.

She laughed as he waved and disappeared into the brush. Sarah was right, he was wicked. But not malicious, she thought, as she turned back to the golden meadow and looked again at Anabelle's grave. Poor thing, shunted off to a corner in disgrace. She was gazing at the marker in a lethargic way when Aaron's voice cut through her thoughts.

"What are you doing here?"

She turned and stared up into his face. "I didn't hear you coming," she accused.

"Maybe I should have warned you."

His footsteps had been muffled by the grass and drowned by the sudden chattering of a colony of ravens in the firs up the hill. She felt as if she'd been caught doing something wrong, and she bristled in self-defense. "Yes, you should have. Unless it's your habit to sneak up on people." He certainly brought out the worst in her, she thought, hearing the wasp-ishness in her voice.

"To sneak.... Is it your habit to intrude into private places?" His dark face and quiet voice filled all the space around her. "*I* have a right to be here."

All at once her anger disappeared, and she regretted trespassing where she didn't belong. He was right, of course, but he was lashing out defensively the same as she. "I'm sorry," she said, spreading her hands, offering an apology, or perhaps sympathy.

Aaron looked at her strangely, as if unable to make out what she was saying. She thought it was probably the first time he'd heard her speak a civil word to him.

"I'm sorry," she repeated. "I just happened upon this place. I...I didn't know what it was. And then...." She stopped. "I wasn't doing any harm."

"No, of course you weren't." His face softened as he saw the freshly watered soil around the flowers. "It's my turn to say I'm sorry." Then, in a flat tone he asked, "What did Coe want? I saw him leaving as I came up. What did he want?"

I don't have to answer your questions, she thought, all the tentative friendliness disappearing with a word. Aloud, she said, "He was on his way to the house to remind us of his party Saturday."

"He came this way to get to the house?" He glared, directing his suspicions at her.

"Well, that's what he said."

"And you didn't believe that. No, of course you didn't." His face hardened again, and the dark blood suffused his cheeks. "He was telling you about my mother, wasn't he?"

They were still standing beside Anabelle's grave, and there was nothing she could say.

"What did he say?" When she didn't answer, he took a step closer. "I asked you a question."

"He didn't tell me anything." Then Winston's words came back to her, and she felt herself blush.

"I knew it."

"He said he wanted to marry her," she hurriedly put in.

"And . . . ?"

"And that she wouldn't have him."

"And that's all?"

"He seemed . . . sad," she said. "Full of regrets."

"Yes, I know." Aaron's eyebrows lifted. "He enjoys playing the brokenhearted faithful follower."

"He didn't seem to be enjoying it," she lied, in spite of having had the same idea herself.

Aaron smiled, and she almost stepped back in surprise. "It gave him a safe reason for never marrying, or even falling in love." Aaron looked down at her, and his face was untroubled for once. "My mother understood that. Someday I'll tell you about her. About her courage, and her spirit, and what they did to it." His thoughts turned inward again, his eyes no longer focused on hers. "But they never broke her. In spite of all of them, she was kind and gentle and loving." He skirted the grave and began to prowl among the stones. "She loved the land. And she taught me to love it, too, and respect it."

His tone dared her to disagree, and she had to. "Daniel says you want to log it all off. Clear cut everything." She followed him up the gently sloping ground toward the stump.

"I keep telling you not to believe everything you hear. Yes, I want to log it. Log it, not rape it. Proper logging won't harm the land. Daniel's way is to get the top dollar today and get out. To hell with tomorrow. You know, thousands of acres—thousands of square miles of forest—were destroyed that way in the early days."

"The old lumber barons?"

He nodded. "But we've learned about land management now. Cutting certain stands and leaving others. Replanting, improving the land. The only excuse for ruining the forests is greed." He looked at her hard. "I suppose Daniel told you he wants to make a park out of it."

She said he had.

"He wants to join with Ed Whirlman. Have you ever seen one of Whirlman's developments?" He rested against the vine-covered remnants of a giant fir, and she sat on a lower stump, looking up at him. Pupil and master. "Let me tell you about Whirlman Development." He described roads cut through the forest and asphalt laid in city blocks; houses shoulder to shoulder, linked by a sinew of rock music from transistor radios. "Ten acres cleared for the pool, and another hundred for the golf course. There would be duplexes and triplexes. And don't forget the convention facilities. A Coney Island with trees. And not too damn many trees, at that."

"It doesn't have to be that way," she protested.

"It does if Ed Whirlman builds it, and that's whom Daniel's dealing with. Or trying to deal with.

He'll get a percentage, shares in the company, if he can get Sarah to sign.'' He sighed, staring at his clenched hands. "As long as she lives, she has complete control of the property.''

"The dead often leave behind a different legacy than they intended,'' she said, thinking of her father.

"Oh, this would have pleased Jacob no end. It was unfair to Daniel to leave him only a share of the proceeds from the collection, and I've offered to take him into the logging as a full partner. But it's not fast enough for him. He wants it all, now.''

"And you want to stop him.''

"Any way I can.''

Any way he can, she thought. Her mind went back to what he'd said about Sarah controlling the property as long as she lived, and from there to Sarah's fall down the stairs. She pushed the thought aside, refusing to explore it any further.

"I know there'll be more and more vacationers coming up to Kulshan,'' Aaron was saying. "The roads are better, and people are more mobile. But they won't turn it into the very thing they're trying to get away from. Not if I can stop it.''

She looked up into his face. "You've given it a lot of thought. You really do love the land.''

His gaze was far away. When he turned to look at her, he hesitated, as if deciding whether or not to go on. With the faintest smile he said, "For years after my mother died, it was the only refuge I had. Only the land and the woods were always warm and welcoming. My mother had tried to teach me not to despair of finding love in the world, but sometimes it seemed like a forlorn hope. Only the land kept it alive.''

In the silence that followed, she said, "I'd like to see it the way you've seen it. With the trees and the animals in full possession."

He smiled down at her. "Someday I'll take you to Little Devil Falls." He blinked then, as if coming out of a dream. "No, I probably won't. Because you won't be here long enough." He stood up, pulling her to her feet, and put his hands on her arms. "I hope you won't be here long enough. I hope you leave here soon, as soon as you can."

"I thought we had that all settled," she said. "I have a job to do."

"I know. Can't you take your notes and finish the job in Seattle?" His grip was so tight on her arms that he shook her as he spoke.

His rapid change of mood frightened her. More than his fingers biting into her flesh or the intensity of his scowl, it was the sudden shift that sent warning signals shooting through her whole being. "I thought you wanted the whole thing scrapped." She tried to back away. She could feel the hair at the back of her head, damp with the heat, standing away from her scalp.

"I don't care what Sarah does, or what she sells. She can sell the faucets out of the bathrooms for all I care." His grip tightened. "I just want you out. Please. Just pack up and go."

"You know I can't do that. And why should I? Because you say so?"

"Yes. I don't suppose that's good enough, but I can't explain."

"And I can't leave just because you want me to. You're hurting my arms." He jerked his hands away.

But fear had driven away the warmth and sympathy she had felt between them. Why couldn't he just stay one way or the other? If he was the monster she thought he was, why did he have to show her these flashes of a gentle loving side? She wanted to see the kind side, to know it. She could still feel the imprint of his hands on her arms, as if she had become extraordinarily sensitive where he had touched her.

She turned away abruptly and hurried down the hill. He let her get as far as the broken gate, then called out to her.

"Wait. I wanted to ask you if you'd seen Floyd."

She stopped, but didn't turn or answer.

"We can't find him anywhere. I thought you might have seen him."

She turned slowly and started back up the slope. She would have to tell him what she had done.

CHAPTER EIGHT

COURTNEY WALKED SLOWLY back up the hill and faced Aaron. He listened impassively as she explained that Floyd had been feeling unhappy and wanted to visit his cousin in Walla Walla. He scowled and shook his head.

"His cousin's eighty-three," Aaron said. "He has barely enough to get by on—and he hates Floyd. Last time Floyd went over there, his cousin called the police to get him off the place."

Courtney didn't understand; Floyd had seemed so happy at the prospect.

"Floyd forgets," Aaron said. "I guess there were happy times—when they were both younger." Together they started back down the slope. "I'll have to go down to Harrington's or Jilly's and see if I can find him before he hitches a ride."

"He didn't seem to have any money," Courtney said. "What does he find to spend his wages on up here?"

The trail headed into the woods just beyond the fenced clearing. They walked single file most of the time, with Aaron in front. They had walked some distance before Aaron said over his shoulder, "Floyd gets room and board and 'walking around' money. The rest of Floyd's wages are paid into a trust fund for his future use."

Courtney was shocked. "Haven't you heard of the Thirteenth Amendment? It freed the slaves." As the trail widened and she drew abreast of him, she said defiantly, "I gave him the bus fare. Loaned it to him." She tossed her head, glad to have shaken him.

He glared at her. "We'll have to hurry. It's not safe for him to be roaming around."

Courtney stopped. She was not going any farther until she knew who was unsafe, and in what way. She didn't know what was wrong, but it didn't make sense to her that a grown man, a big strong man like Floyd, was in danger. Aaron went on a step or two, then stopped and turned back to her. As he did, she saw the concern and anger in his face, and she was sorry she hadn't just pretended everything was fine until they got to the house.

It suddenly occurred to her that perhaps it was unsafe for Aaron to have Floyd out and "roaming around." She didn't have any notion of what kind of danger Floyd could pose for Aaron, but she didn't doubt that it was possible. In the seconds before Aaron spoke, Courtney realized how isolated they were, how far from everyone. That was how it was on the mountain—five minutes from the house and you were all alone, away from companions and advice—and help.

It was too late now to pretend everything was all right. "In what way isn't it safe?"

Aaron stared at her almost as if he were too angry to speak, and she quailed. Or perhaps he was making a judgment about how much to tell her.

"It's Floyd," he said at last with an air of resignation. "I didn't want to tell you because some people foolishly get upset. And there's no need to."

"Well, if you don't tell me, I'll never know whether I'm upset or not, will I?" She had thought he was in some kind of a hurry, and now there was all this hemming and hawing. "What about Floyd?"

"He's slow. Marginally retarded. There's nothing to be afraid of; he's not going to hurt anyone. But the boys down at Jilly's tease him. They'll take his money away from him, and that's not so bad, but they think up wonderful little stunts for him from time to time. He can't remember to be suspicious of their schemes because they laugh and play up to him." He sighed. "He thinks they're being friendly."

"This has happened before?"

"Of course. Did you think you were the first one to get him into trouble?" He smiled at her. "Are you coming?"

They started back along the trail. He said Floyd had been judged untrainable until he got to a state hospital with a good rehabilitation program. "He's not young, you know. Forty years ago, when he was a boy, it was common to put everyone who didn't— or couldn't—act the way the majority acted into the same...pen." He had come to Rockhurst along with another trainee as part of a work-release program.

That didn't jibe with everything Courtney had heard about Jacob Padgett. "It was your grand-father who brought them here?"

Aaron turned and looked her straight in the eye. "It was very cheap labor."

She closed her eyes and turned her head. The day was suddenly chilly. After a moment she said, "Sure-ly Floyd is free to leave now if he wants to."

"Of course. Legally. But I worry about his surviving. . . on the outside. The hospital taught the boys how to work and earn money, but they didn't teach them how to use it. And his notions of ownership and private property are—" he shook his head "—somewhat vague, to say the least."

They moved silently along a narrow stretch of the woodsy trail, where the salal branches reached out to clutch at passersby. When Aaron stopped and waited for her to catch up, they were still under the canopy of fir, but through the trees they could see the wide lawns rolling out in front of Rockhurst.

"For a quiet little thing," he said when she was standing beside him, "you seem to get people to tell you a lot. More than they intended sometimes, I'm sure. And you get into all sorts of corners that don't concern you." He gazed steadily at her, his eyes tracing the cap of dark curls, then staunchly lifted chin and the cheeks glowing with the heat. "And your face is dirty." He reached out and rubbed a smudge from the bridge of her nose, and burst into laughter.

She had seen him laugh only once before, and she had forgotten how it changed his face. The sun shone on his bronze skin, warming it to a golden glow. The muscles in his neck rippled and his teeth flashed. She had forgotten, too, how his laughter had affected her, making her want to laugh with him. . . and want to touch him.

"You're worse than that raccoon," Aaron said. "I'm not surprised you both got yourselves locked in the tower." He laughed again.

Courtney's face flamed with more than the heat of the day. What a fool she was! She had been attracted by his laughter—and it was directed at her. His mercurial changes of mood were bad enough, but this was too much. He was abusive, laughing at her. She tried to walk away from him, but the ground was rough, and he merely lengthened his stride to keep up with her. He stepped in front of her and blocked the way. "Wait, please. I didn't mean to offend you."

"You go from shouting to laughing at me, and you didn't mean to offend me? What is it supposed to do? Make me feel wonderful?"

"No, of course not. I'm sorry." He raised a hand as if to brush more dust off her cheek, but stopped. "Besides, I haven't shouted at you all day." He scowled at her. "Have I?"

He was blocking her way, and he was so big, she couldn't even see around him. He could keep them there all day if he didn't move. But she sensed there was no belligerence in his stance. He was making an offer—if not of friendship, at least of a truce. And if she didn't accept it, there might never be another chance. Besides, she thought with some surprise, she'd like to be friends with Aaron. Yes, she'd like that very much.

She shrugged and said, "I guess I have been a nuisance."

"Never a nuisance." He smiled down at her, and she felt a strange flutter in her heart. "But certainly full of surprises. And good for us."

Her eyes opened wide in surprise.

"Everyone at Rockhurst has been happier since you came. Jenny feels appreciated for once. Floyd has found a companion. Sarah. . .Sarah has someone to talk to. It's lonely up here for her."

Courtney was pleased to know that he had noticed life was hard for other people. She basked in this unexpected praise and hadn't—couldn't—get enough. "And you? Are you happier?"

His eyes smiled into hers. "I don't remember when I've laughed, before you came." His arms wrapped around her. "Yes, I'm happy now that you're here." His embrace tightened as he bent his head to kiss her. His lips were soft and warm, searching, seeking, hungry for an answer.

And she answered him. Her lips met his, and she slid her arms around his neck. Her body molded itself to his, and every nerve was aware of his touch. Her blood pounded in her ears, and she felt dizzy. She knew that all the rest of her life, the smell of fir would bring back the memory of this soaring happiness.

It was like coming home, so perfectly did their spirits meet—and, at the same time, like a rocket to the moon. Her knees were weak, and when he released her, she would have fallen had he not been holding her.

With his arms still around her, he moved his head back to look at her. His face was serious. "Courtney—"

"Please." She put her fingertips to his lips. "Don't say anything. It's...." It wasn't really sudden, or even unexpected, she realized now. But the moment was perfect in itself. She didn't want to hear protestations of love, or attraction, or whatever it was. For she would want to believe them...and what if it was just play to him?

"Just don't say a word."

He kissed the fingertips resting against his lips and smiled. "All right. For now."

She stepped back clear of his arms and immediately wished she hadn't. There was a time to be sensible—and it always came too soon.

He took her hand lightly and turned toward the house. "Come on, we'll go in search of our wandering boy." He glanced at her. "That is, if you'd like to."

His diffidence, as if he expected to be rebuffed, touched her. It was another of those odd contradictions that made him so fascinating. He obviously ran Rockhurst, even if he wasn't the official head of the household, and he had a reputation as a tartar. Yet he was strangely constrained in his personal approach. She wondered what made him so hesitant.

When they got to the house, they found that Daniel had left, taking the station wagon, and Courtney offered the use of her car. She went upstairs to get the keys and a jacket, for Aaron had said it would be dark before they got back.

In her room, she grabbed a beige corduroy jacket, checked her purse for the keys and went to the big dark dresser to comb her hair. As she bent closer to the mirror, she saw an envelope propped up among the jars and combs and scarves littering the top. It was smudged and much folded; the edges were foxed and furry. There was no name on the outside, and inside only a piece of paper, equally worn and crumpled, except for the righthand edge, where the jagged outline looked freshly torn. It seemed to be a short list of some sort, in Jacob Padgett's handwriting. Puzzling over it, she tapped the envelope against her cheek and caught a strong whiff of gasoline, or motor oil.

She knew then that Floyd had placed the envelope there. He had evidently meant to give her this list before he left. But why? What did it mean? She looked at Jacob's spidery handwriting again. It was a list of book titles. *Vanity Fair*. *Pride and Prejudice*. *A Tale of Two Cities*. They meant nothing to her except as titles of books she had read and enjoyed. Old books, classics. Was it Floyd's reading list? That didn't seem likely if, as Aaron had said, Floyd was a slow learner

If, as Aaron had said. Slowly, with a sick feeling, she crumpled the list and shoved it into her jacket pocket. She turned and left the room, forgetting to fix her hair, forgetting to close the door. Mechanically, she walked down the stairs, her mind churning with the realization that she had only Aaron's word that Floyd had been raised in an institution, that he had been wrongly hospitalized.

The stairs, with their deep rose-strewn carpeting, were silent. The house had a quiet, empty feeling, although she knew Sarah and Jenny were in the parlor. It was such a big house, so well insulated against noise and disturbance, that she had come upstairs and down again without anyone knowing. She would be going with Aaron into the quickening dusk—without anyone knowing. She reached the main central hall and stood at the foot of the stairs a moment. What did it matter whether anyone knew where she was? She'd be safe; she'd be with Aaron. Providing it *was* safe to be with Aaron, a small voice within her said.

This was ridiculous, she told herself firmly. There was no way that Aaron was going to harm her. In the few seconds it took to cross to the back hallway, she relived the golden moment at the edge of the forest. She could still smell the fir needles crushed under their feet. With a half smile she wondered what he would have said if she hadn't stopped him, and briefly regretting having done it.

It was the first time, except for brief snatches, that she'd ever been alone with him. And she had succumbed in those few moments to his personality and the sun—and his laughter.

She suddenly realized that whenever she was alone with him, or whenever he talked to her, she began to believe everything he said. He had convinced her to work at the little desk in the alcove. He said the tower door had fallen shut. And, against her common sense, she had begun to believe it. He said Floyd had been in a mental institution—and without proof, she believed it. Was she a lamb being led by a rare brilliant smile and a firm voice to the slaughter?

She shivered, wishing some other word had presented itself. Nevertheless, she was buying wholesale what Aaron said because he was big and bronze and strong. Because he had kissed her in the sunshine. Was it a Judas kiss?

She stood on the back step for a moment, holding the screen door open, and tried to shake off her fancies. Looking up, she saw Aaron standing beside her VW across the yard. The sun touched his cheek with gold, and her heart jumped at the sight.

But remember, the small voice said, *you don't know that anything he says is true.*

Aaron hadn't moved. His face was still set toward the south, his jaw tight, the lines between his eyes deep. But his whole being had taken on a sinister aspect. The scowl was cruel, the jaw ruthless.

Oh, God, why was she so confused? It was frightening. She had no control over anything—nothing that happened, no one around her. And now she had no control over even her own thoughts and feelings. Even as she looked, things changed shape and meaning until she didn't know what was real and what was fantasy.

There was nothing to do but go forward into the nightmare and see what happened. She looked with regret at Aaron and what might have been, then squared her shoulders. She let the screen door go, and it slapped shut behind her. The sound brought Aaron's gaze to her and he watched, smiling, as she crossed the dusty yard.

Her steps grew slower as she got nearer the car. Aaron's smile faded, and he cocked his head.

"Are you all right?"

"Yes, of course," she said. "Why wouldn't I be? Here're the keys." She took them from her pocket and tossed them across the hood of the car to him. He caught them, then came around and opened the passenger door. "Okay. Let's go find that rascal." When she hesitated, he said, "Aren't you coming?"

"No." Her voice squeaked. "I mean, why do you need me?"

"Well, I don't exactly need you. I thought...." His eyes widened as they searched her face.

She felt her heart—her world—plunge sickeningly as he said, "I see." Pain and sorrow washed across his face, instantly hidden by the mask of indifference. He stood staring at her for a long moment. She was too weak, too sick to say a word. "Your affections don't last long, do they?" There was no bitterness, only sorrow, in his voice.

She thought she heard her heart break.

He was gone, spraying dust from the drive, almost out of sight before she found the strength to move again.

IT WAS QUITE LATE when Aaron and Floyd returned, but the women, Sarah, Jenny and Courtney, were still up, waiting to hear what had happened. Grinning sheepishly, Floyd stomped into the parlor, where they were waiting. He stood and let Sarah scold him for being an ungrateful foolish wretch, torn between chagrin and excitement at his exploits.

Aaron leaned against the doorjamb, arms crossed, and watched Floyd take his punishment. It occurred to Courtney that they all seemed to be enjoying it: Sarah indulging the chance to be the matriarch. Jenny relishing seeing someone else get called down. Even Floyd reveled in being the center of attention.

"Tell Miss Courtney what happened to her forty dollars, Floyd," Aaron said from the doorway.

"Aw. Them boys beat me out of it." He hung his head and looked at Courtney from under his heavy eyebrows. "I didn't mean to lose it."

"Of course you didn't." She thought it was cruel of Aaron to rub it in that way.

"It was the crookedest game I ever saw," Aaron said. "A new poker variation they made up on the spot—and kept changing to fit the circumstances."

He pushed himself off the wall and strolled over to Courtney, counting out money as he came. "They were so sorry to have fooled Floyd, they insisted on returning their winnings."

Floyd guffawed. "Aaron shook it outten them."

Aaron pushed the money into Courtney's hand. "It isn't mine, it wasn't theirs, and it certainly wasn't Floyd's." Reluctantly she accepted the money, and Aaron said, "I think that about wraps it up, Floyd."

"You ain't sending me back to the hospital, are you?"

Sarah sighed loudly. "Floyd, every time you run away, you ask if we're going to send you back. We haven't sent you back yet, have we?"

"You're not goods bought at a store, Floyd." Aaron put his hand on Floyd's arm. "We're not going to send you back."

At the tone of dismissal, Floyd breathed a sigh of relief and turned to leave. He stopped beside Courtney's chair. "You find...." He stopped and waggled his eyebrows in an obvious signal to be discreet. She nodded and murmured that she had. Floyd grinned with satisfaction and left the room in higher spirits than Courtney would have expected. It seemed to Courtney that she was the only one at Rockhurst to retire that night in less than high good humor.

She threw herself on her bed, wide-eyed, sleepless, and achingly unhappy. There had been not the slightest sign from Aaron that they had kissed in the sunlight. Or that she had betrayed his trust by being afraid. He wasn't even angry. Surely that meant the end of all hope for her. Aaron was indifferent, as if her lack of faith, her callous behavior, were unimportant to him. He simply didn't care.

Or had she hurt him so badly that he didn't dare show it? Either way, she knew it was too late for her. She turned her pillow over, pounding it into submission, and tried again to close her eyes. But the scene in the yard, where she and Aaron had stared at each other beside the VW, kept coming back. It wasn't until he'd spoken those words, in a weary flat voice—"Your affections don't last long, do they?"—that she'd realized fully and with a shock, that she loved him. She'd known it in the instant of pain that crossed his face. Even then, when she hadn't known if he had engineered her entrapment in the tower, or was planning to steal Sarah's legacy, she'd known she loved him.

This was nothing like what she had felt for Ken. And certainly nothing like anything else she had ever known, for there were no reservations now. If she was afraid of him, that was too bad for her, for whatever he was, whatever he might do, she loved him.

Sometime during the night, she considered packing up and leaving Rockhurst in the morning. It would be easier. She wouldn't be subjected to Aaron's indifference, to being close to him, talking to him, touching him and knowing he didn't care. But she knew she couldn't leave while Sarah needed her. Courtney thought bitterly that she herself was still the only one who could be trusted—the only one between Sarah and the ravens who would steal her inheritance. A picture of Aaron's dark face, his hair and eyes as black as a raven's feathers, came to her.

Was he one of them? She didn't know, and it didn't matter. She had to stay and help Sarah, even if, or perhaps because, she loved him.

And she had driven him away. Always her heart returned to that wounding knowledge. In despair, she turned her face to the wall and stared at the moonlight shadows until they faded in the light of dawn.

THE NEXT DAY she came down to the kitchen late, red-eyed, exhausted, tense and nervous. Jenny was just coming in from the garden, carrying a half-bushel basket of string beans. Her face was flushed, and tendrils of damp hair clung to her cheeks. Heat had wilted her house dress and apron so that they hung limply against her spare frame.

Courtney held the kitchen door further open as Jenny gave the screen door a thump with her hip. Courtney stood a moment listening to a colony of ravens chattering in the firs behind the house.

"Spreading scandal," Jenny said scornfully. "And bad news."

Courtney laughed. "Why not happy news?"

"I don't know why not. Because they're scavengers, I guess. Waiting for the leavings. Looking to steal what ain't theirs." She cast a look of loathing toward the stand of firs and moved on into the kitchen. She set her basket on the scrubbed wooden table in the center of the room. "Beans is out of the rabbits' reach," she said, "but it seems like they all come on at once." She looked with distaste at the heaping basket. "Too hot for canning; I'm going to freeze 'em. But you got to do 'em up right away, else you might as well be buying that three-day-old stuff from Harrington's." She picked the basket up and carried it to the sink. "Well. I got no choice but to do 'em."

"Would it be. could I help you?" Courtney crossed to the iron sink. Her mind was in too much turmoil to concentrate on her own work today, anyway. Helping Jenny would be a diversion.

"I guess any fool can cut 'em and wash 'em." Jenny glanced sideways at Courtney. "Well, at least wash your hands first."

For the next hour Courtney worked happily beside Jenny, her mind occupied enough to hold misery at bay. She had the delicious sensation of playing hooky, because Sarah wouldn't approve of her spending the morning in the kitchen instead of at her desk. But Sarah was unlikely to come down before lunch, giving Courtney plenty of time to talk to Jenny. Jenny would know all about Aaron, and the enigma of his character. . . if she'd unbend enough to tell Courtney about him. Diffidently, Courtney suggested that Jenny knew all about everyone at Rockhurst. At least everyone who'd been there long.

"As much as I care to know, I guess." She glanced at Courtney. "I'm not much for tending other people's business."

"Oh, I know you're not," Courtney went on, doggedly ignoring the implied warning. "But someone who's been here forever, like Aaron, for instance, you couldn't help knowing all about him." When Jenny didn't answer, Courtney prodded, 'At least I guess he's been here a long time."

Jenny turned on the faucet and let the water splash over a colander of cut beans, sorting through them with one hand and picking out a blossom and a stem end that had fallen in.

"Was he born here," Courtney asked when Jenny had turned off the water, "or did he come to Rockhurst from somewhere else?"

"No, he didn't come from somewhere else. Daniel was born back east, but Aaron was born here." She made an odd sound in her throat that might have been a laugh. "Yes, indeedy, he was sure enough born here. Stirred up trouble then and never did quit."

There was a pause while Jenny filled a large pan with water and set it on the great black stove that dominated one side of the kitchen. "That'll be boiling by the time we finish these beans. Then you can set up the boxes and bags while I tend to the blanching."

Apparently, Courtney thought, Jenny considered the packing boxes a noncritical step that even Courtney couldn't spoil.

"So Aaron was born here," Courtney said as she set up the boxes on the center table. "And Anabelle was his mother. Who was his father?"

"We'd of all liked to of known that. At the time, anyways. Don't much matter now, one way or the other. She's dead, and most likely he is, too."

"I guess...I guess that's what makes Aaron so.... He seems so unhappy. So lonely." Courtney was appalled, hearing herself probe so shamelessly into Aaron's affairs, but she didn't seem able to stop.

"Well, if he's lonely, being a bastard ain't the reason." Jenny gave Courtney a sly glance and snickered. "Half the people on this mountain couldn't tell you for sure who their daddy was. Not with absolute certainty."

"Come on, Jenny."

Jenny came as close to laughing as Courtney had ever seen. "S'true. And they grew up okay." She turned back to her work at the sink. "Not that Aaron ain't okay, you understand. He's not very...sociable. But he's steady, if you know what I mean. Steady as a rock, is what Aaron is."

And handsome and strong and tender, Courtney added silently. And perhaps as cold as steel. "He seems so angry all the time."

"Angry? Lordy, you ain't seen him angry. When he gets mad, he hollers the house down. He ain't no silent sufferer, if that's what you're thinking." Her hands stopped in midair as she was about to add another colanderful of beans to the pot. "Well, maybe he is. But not when he's mad. Aaron'll always let you know what he's thinking.... No, that ain't right, either." She stopped and considered. "What it is, you know whether he likes something or don't like it."

"Yes, I'm all too familiar with that."

"Yeah. But you don't always know *why* he likes it or don't like it." She tipped the beans into the boiling water, then set a small yellow timer and put it on top of the oven. "But he's okay, you understand. It's just that...well, there wasn't no good fairy around to bring Aaron up."

She went to the sink and stared out the window. It was as if the past was out there, shimmering in the brutal sun. "From before he was born, he didn't have no chance for a normal home. Rockhurst wasn't no more normal then than it is now. And Anabelle had sense enough to try to get away. Lit out the day she turned eighteen.''

Anabelle had taken the bus to Seattle, Jenny said, and there she had met a sailor. That was all Anabelle had ever told them about him, except that he was shipped out a few weeks later. ''In about six months, Miss Anabelle comes home with her souvenir in her belly.''

Jacob had been furious. Anabelle had been his darling, his prize, and she had not only run away from him, she had given herself to another man. ''And what Jacob owned wasn't supposed to try and get free. He never forgave her for that.''

She had come home because she wasn't well enough to take care of herself, and she wasn't strong enough to run off again. Jacob had seen to it that there was no money available. As Jenny spoke, Courtney thought of all the valuables, the silver and the icons Anabelle could have smuggled out and traded for help. But the house had become an armed camp. Everyone was set to spying on everyone else.

''My own ma was living here with me then, sick, waiting to die. So I couldn't help Anabelle, or I'd've lost my job and the only place I had to take care of Ma.''

So that was the hold that had kept Jenny here in those years, Courtney thought. Jacob had known well the uses of blackmail and extortion.

''I used to think about going to Seattle and doing war work, taking Ma with me. But it was hard. I'd save up the money for the fare and maybe a month's rent, and Ma'd get an attack—she used to get awful sick." She shook her head. "I just . . . it was too hard. Then Anabelle got in trouble, and there was the baby."

Courtney asked if anyone else had tried to help Anabelle.

"Who was there? Me, Sarah, the hired man. He sure couldn't do anything."

"What about Sarah?" Courtney asked. "Couldn't she help her stepdaughter?"

"She did what she could. Sarah had real feeling for Anabelle, in spite of Anabelle's being Jacob's pet, and Sarah's not being able to have a chick of her own. That might've put some women off Anabelle, but not Sarah."

There was nothing she could do, Jenny said. Jacob had suspected Sarah of helping Anabelle to run away the first time. And he suspected her of having some plans of her own, so he punished her, too.

"He never raised a hand to her, of course. But there's some things worse than a beating." She sighed. "She just kept all them clothes ready, but she never did get a chance to use them."

After the baby was born, Anabelle had never regained her strength, and lived only until Aaron was six. But in those years, Anabelle had given Aaron all the love she'd never had herself.

"But you said she was Jacob's pet, his darling."

"That ain't love, girl. Being cosseted and showed off and bragged on, and never. . . . I don't know how to say things, but it's like he never really *looked* at her. You know what I mean? Or maybe it's that he didn't listen to her, I don't know. But he didn't no more know that girl than a possum knows how to fly."

And so Anabelle lavished her love on her baby. "And kindness," Jenny said. "Like she was trying to teach him to be kind to every living thing, and you know that ain't really...practical. There's a lot of God's creatures that don't warrant kindness, not being so all-fired wonderful themselves."

Courtney wondered briefly if that was why Aaron wouldn't lie in wait at dawn to shoot the rabbits that ate Jenny's vegetable garden. But perhaps that was too fanciful, she thought. Then, with a heart-chilling shock, it came to her that perhaps yesterday in the sunshine, with the birds fluttering in the firs, Aaron had kissed her to be kind. Courtney swayed from the blow, clutching the table edge to keep from falling. She forced the thought away, refusing to deal with it, and commanded herself to listen to Jenny.

"Anabelle says to me one time," Jenny was saying, "that she knew there wasn't no way on earth to keep all the meanness in the world from getting to her baby. But when it did, she wanted him to know deep down inside himself that there was love in the world, too." She shook her head. "I don't know where she got such notions."

Like an exclamation point to her words, the timer sounded, and Jenny pulled the wire basket from the water and plunged it with its cargo of blanched beans into a huge pan of cold water. As she swished the basket around in the cold bath, rinsing and chilling the beans, Courtney asked her how Jacob had treated Anabelle's baby. Jacob was neither kind nor unkind most of time, Jenny said, but hardly interested. The only time he seemed to notice the boy was if he acted up or showed too much spirit.

"Then the old man had a way to quieten him down. He'd say, 'Remember, boy, you're here through my generosity.' S'wonder the very word didn't choke the old hypocrite. Anyways, he'd say, 'You are your mother's shame and sorrow. You better think about trying to erase that a little, instead of making it worse.' "

Courtney stared at her, speechless. "I can't...I never heard of anything so...." She thought of Aaron's furrowed brow and wanted to kiss away the hurt.

"You can bless your lucky stars you ain't never run into anyone like Jacob." She pulled the basket of beans from the chill bath. "You got them boxes ready?" Speaking half to herself as she shook beans from the basket into the boxes, she said, "Seemed like after Jacob died, we'd finally get some peace in the house. But that was before...." Her voice trailed off.

"Before what?"

Jenny looked at Courtney for a moment as if deciding whether to go on or not. Then she shrugged and said, "Before we saw that Jacob's spirit was gonna still be here. I don't mean like a ghost or nothing like that. I mean it just seems like there was too much meanness to die all at once." She looked up, her gaze traveling around the room as if she could see through the ceiling and the walls to the rest of the house. "It's still hanging around. Turning everything sour and black. Just as if Jacob was still here."

CHAPTER NINE

COURTNEY SHARED JENNY'S OPINION about the influence of Jacob Padgett. His shadow hung over the house like smoke from a distant fire. Rockhurst breathed in malevolence and exhaled distrust and suspicion. Shakespeare had said something, she remembered, about the evil men do, and certainly Jacob's evil lived on after him. She wondered if there was any good interred with his bones. The more she heard of him, the more she doubted it.

The unhappiness and disquiet all around drained her energy. So, too, did her silent concern about Sarah's safety. For, with no one around she dared talk to, she found her mind mulling over the situation instead of concentrating on her work. Even so, she almost welcomed the effort of worrying and puzzling over Sarah, the treasure, and the Padgett inheritance, for it kept her thoughts off the misery that seemed to be the only result of her love for Aaron. There were times when, relaxed and thinking herself at ease, her mind would turn a corner, and she would find herself again going over that afternoon, those few moments with Aaron. She knew, now that it was too late, how she felt about Aaron, but she had no way to judge what his actions toward her meant. When she first came to Rockhurst, she had promised Daniel that she would come to him with any problem, but now she was reluctant to do that. Daniel was too charming, too ready to oblige for her to have faith in his ability to understand.

And if she had wanted to confide in Daniel, how could she describe her problem? "Your cousin hardly speaks to me." Or, "I never see Aaron anymore." For those were the only visible signs of her unhappiness, the dismal remains of those precious moments when Aaron had laughed with her and said she was good for them and kissed her. He avoided her now whenever possible, and when he was forced to endure her presence, he was distant and cool. Not that he was around very often. He worked from dawn to dark in the woods, and since Samantha Coe had returned, he spent the evenings out somewhere with her. Courtney's life at Rockhurst had become a torture, and daily it became more of an effort to go on about her job, keeping up the listing, the pricing and sorting.

It was with real relief, then, that she looked forward to Winston Coe's party on Saturday. The whole house was stirring with the preparations. Sarah was atwitter with anticipation, and by Thursday afternoon, Jenny had steamed and pressed the cranberry crepe dress.

"Are you planning to spend the next two days getting ready for that party of Winston's?" Aaron asked at dinner. "All so we can go over and let the city folks see the hillbillies?"

"Now, Aaron, dear, it isn't like that at all," Sarah cooed. "You know Winston invites us because we're his friends." Her high voice was gently admonishing. "You know he likes you—and Daniel, and me."

"Oh, I believe he likes you, all right, you old flirt."

"Aaron, stop that." But it was plain that she was pleased.

"You laugh at his jokes and gasp at his exploits and make him feel like a regular devil, don't you?" Aaron teased her.

"I listen politely when I'm spoken to, if that's what you mean."

Aaron whooped, and Daniel grinned across the table at Courtney.

"You old fraud, it probably does you both a world of good," Aaron went on. "But I'll be darned if I know why Daniel and I are needed."

"*I* enjoy Winston's parties," Daniel said.

Aaron lifted an eyebrow.

"Now don't start fussing again, you two," Sarah said. "I can hardly go by myself, Aaron. I need both of you there. And this year, we have Courtney to look out for, too, you know."

Yes, Courtney thought, she wouldn't miss it for the world. It had occurred to her that a party, where people relaxed and let go of their inhibitions, might offer just the conditions she needed. There, amid the strange faces and laughter and music, perhaps someone, Aaron or Daniel or Winston himself, would let slip the one word that would lead her to some answers. Answers about the treasure—or about Aaron.

For the first time in days, Aaron's eyes met hers. "Yes, we do have to look out for Courtney, don't we?" She felt her face flush as he turned to Sarah. "Well, you know full well I'll go to the party. But I don't see any need to turn the whole house upside down for it. Jenny has enough to do without asking her to be a tailor and ladies' maid and goodness knows what else besides."

Jenny's "Hah!" was muffled by the clatter of her tray cracking against the swinging door to the kitchen.

In spite of Aaron's objections, the house remained in turmoil for the next two days. On Saturday, Sarah's hair still had to be shampooed and set, the station wagon washed and polished, hem lengths given their final adjustment.

"Sarah wouldn't be caught dead in the pickup at that party tonight, even if Floyd had got it to running right," Jenny told Courtney as they had a cup of midmorning coffee. When Jenny had drained her cup, she pushed it aside and turned once again to rehemming the skirt of the cranberry crepe dress with tiny even stitches.

"She really makes a thing of this party," Courtney said.

"Highlight of her year." Jenny held the skirt up to check the lay of the material. "Jacob would never take her, but it was the only place he'd let her go alone. 'Course the Boys always went with her." She bit the thread off. "You ain't made much fuss about what you're gonna wear. Not like some people."

Courtney explained with a laugh that there wasn't much to fuss about since she had brought along only one good outfit "just in case," a long gray and white skirt and a sleeveless gray top.

Jenny offered to press it for her, reckoning she'd look 'as cool as a block of ice.' Getting up, Jenny circled the big scrubbed table and went to the window. Leaning on the sink, she peered out at the backyard. "Wish that fool Floyd'd hurry up and finish polishing the wagon. He's got to sweep inside, too, and I don't suppose that would ever occur to him without I tell him to do it.''

Welcoming the excuse to talk to Floyd, Courtney offered to deliver the message. He seemed always to be lurking around, waiting for her to say something, and for nearly a week she had been trying to see him alone. But remembering his obvious signal for caution and discretion, the right time had never come.

Now she found him rubbing the right front fender of the wagon. The maroon paint glowed with wax. He stepped back to take a look, then bent forward, breathed onto the fender and polished briefly again.

"You can see yourself in it," she said as she came up to him.

"Jesus God, don't creep up on people that way." Floyd wiped his face with the polishing cloth. "'Scuse my French, but you nearly scairt me outta ten years' growth.''

"I'm sorry. I didn't mean to startle you. I didn't know you were concentrating so hard.''

"Well, it ain't so much a matter of concentrating as it is of always being on tenterhooks around here.'' He looked around as if expecting someone to come at him from the shadows of the barn. "Don't tell no one I barked at you like that, will you?''

"I won't. I came to tell you Jenny said you should be sure to sweep out the inside of the car.''

"Geez." He spat in disgust. "Wouldn't that frost you, though? She thinks I'm some kind of dumbbell or something.''

Courtney grinned at him sympathetically. It was the kind of unnecessary order Rudi Broberg was always giving her, and she knew how Floyd felt. For a moment she watched him rubbing the fender, feeling the sun loosening some of the knots in her shoulders. Even at this early morning hour, it was beating down on the red dust and shimmering in the distance.

"Floyd...about those book titles...."

He looked at her blankly.

"The list you left in my room."

"Oh, that there paper—that was a paper of Old Man Padgett's wasn't it?"

"Yes, it was his handwriting."

"But all it was was names of books?" He seemed disappointed.

"Yes. You can't read, can you, Floyd?"

"Of course I can read." He attacked the polishing vigorously. After a moment, he added in a mumble, "I can read printing. Can't read writing."

It had never occurred to Courtney before to wonder about the handicap of Floyd's intelligence. She had just accepted the fact that he needed some extra direction, but she hadn't thought what that might mean to him in his daily life. She reached out to him, then let her hand fall helplessly to her side. What could she say to this great lanky man with a child's mind? She turned away, overwhelmed at the thought of how Jacob had taken advantage of him, and of Floyd's frustration.

He called her back, in a low urgent whisper that interrupted her musings. She looked quickly around the yard, put on the alert by the tone of his voice. She saw that they were still alone, but Floyd's whisper made it clear he wanted to take no chances of being overheard.

"Listen, I know that list is important. On account of where I found it." He looked around the vacant yard again.

"Yes?" she said expectantly.

"Not now," Floyd said impatiently. "They'll all be out here before long to see is the wagon ready. And I ain't got the other part with me right here anyhow. The other half of the list."

"You tore it in half?" That explained the ragged edge.

"No, it come that way. Old Man Padgett did that. Sly, he was, and meaner than—"

"Yes, I know. But what about the list?"

"You come out to the barn tomorrow morning and I'll prove to you that I know what I'm talking about. I don't know what the treasure is, or where it is, but I got a pretty good idea of how to find it."

He peered at her while she tried to make sense out of his statement. She didn't want to meet him somewhere—anywhere. All her instincts were against it. But in the morning, in broad daylight, and just at the barn. . . . Her glance went up to take in the big white-trimmed building. There was nothing menacing about it. And she had to know what the treasure was. If knowing could help get Sarah out of here, away from the danger that Courtney felt she was in. . . .

"Everybody'll sleep late tomorrow on account of the party tonight," Floyd said when she didn't answer immediately. "So you meet me about eight o'clock." He thrust his chin out at her. "You just wait right inside the door. No need to come poking around inside." he added, glaring at her suspiciously.

The words, "No need to come inside" were just what she needed to hear. "I'll be there," she said.

THAT NIGHT the station wagon's maroon paint gleamed. The hood reflected the shadows of the firs and the watchful moon behind its veil of haze from the distant forest fire. Sarah sat forward on the front seat, chirping comments and urging Aaron to "just leave the car" as he tried to squeeze between the cars parked along the old logging road leading to Winston Coe's house. She seemed to vibrate with excitement and pleasure, and Courtney hoped she wouldn't fly all to pieces before they arrived.

As Winston greeted them at the door, however, Sarah had her feelings under control. She made him bend to kiss her, then she glided into the room with a gracious smile and a tiny hand extended to a tall, wasted-looking young man with long wavy blond hair, who exclaimed, "Ah, there she is, our lady of the mountains."

As Courtney waited for Daniel to bring her vodka and tonic, she watched Sarah twitter off into the crowd. There were thirty or forty people moving slowly through the room, making that strange, exciting music of a party—the men's voices sounding the bass and tenor, the women the middle tones, with here and there a high sparkling soprano note. A sudden burst of laughter came from the brass section, and a viola cried, "Darling, there you are." Orchestra and chorus came together as patterns shifted and new groups formed.

"I don't know how much of this is vodka and how much is tonic," Daniel said, holding a glass out to her. "Would you believe Winston's hired Barney, the bartender from Jilly's tavern? He's more used to opening a bottle of beer than mixing drinks."

She sipped tentatively, assuring Daniel that the drink was just fine. It would be, as soon as the ice melted, and in the meantime holding it gave her something to do with her hands. Her father's face flashed through her mind and she put on her "Smile, make them like you" look as Daniel said, "The first person I want you to meet is. . . ."

She never heard the name, or any of the ten or fifteen others that were introduced to her during the evening. She agreed with each of the guests as they said ritually, "Isn't this a lovely place? Winston has such exquisite taste," and answered the invariable question, "What are you doing up here in the woods?"

The only variation was an occasional reference to the latest newscast, which had reported on the forest fire. A few of the visitors were nervous about it, but to most it provided a delicious kind of thrill with no real possibility of danger. The locals merely said that things were all right as long as it stayed on the east side. Or, as Tom Harrington said, "If she crosses the summit and starts down, it's time to pull on your boots, boys, and take off."

By the end of the first hour, she had been introduced to a good many people and could navigate her way through the groups on her own. She began to listen not so much to the words said to her, but to the words said to the party. The phrases sounded familiar, and she began to see familiar-looking faces, too. Not really faces she'd seen before, but "party faces"—some amused, some bored, appraising or flirtatious. Eyes restlessly scanning the room for newcomers, or jealously following someone across the room...as hers did, she realized, when she saw Samantha. Looking superb in a cream tunic over pencil-slim pants, Winston's cousin was herding Aaron away from the crowd and into a secluded corner. Not really herding him, Courtney admitted with a pang; he seemed to be following her quite willingly, and she knew that not even the beautiful Samantha could get Aaron to go anywhere he didn't want to go.

She turned her attention to the man who was running a fingertip up and down her arm and asking if she lived in the neighborhood.

She was about to say, yes, she lived here with her sister the nun and her three brothers, who were all wrestlers. But as she looked up, she saw Aaron, alone now, standing in a nearby doorway, his angry gaze boring through the man's back. She suppressed a grin. If Aaron wanted to stand around scowling, he could be of some use at the same time. "You see that tall dark man over there?"

The man turned. "The mean-looking one glaring at me?"

"That's the one. I live with him."

"Oh. Yes, well." The man backed away. "Well, it's a nice party, isn't it? Have a good time." He eased off, with Aaron's eyes still following him. Laughing to herself, she moved across the room toward him. But by the time she reached the doorway, Aaron had disappeared. When she realized he was gone, her chin went up as if in response to a slap. Well, if he was avoiding her, she thought angrily, she'd see that he didn't have to try very hard. She'd keep out of his way, and he could spend his time following Samantha around like a trained poodle. She couldn't care less, she told herself, refusing to listen to the small voice that said she cared too much.

Determined to put Aaron out of her thoughts, at least for a few minutes, she joined a group that was staring up at Winston's huge blue-and-green Thomas Hallman.

"Pure form. The very essence of form."

"And the power, my dear. You can absolutely feel the power."

"Mmm. It works. It works very well."

What they said was true enough of the shapes and play of color in the painting, but it seemed to Courtney she had heard those very words at every gallery opening her father had ever dragged her to. Why didn't someone say it a new way once in a while? She shifted from the group and found herself beside the pale young man with the long wavy blond hair. He had a drink in one long thin hand, and the other, with one finger tentatively outstretched, was hovering over the delicately detailed bronze wolf.

"So deliciously primitive," he murmured.

She nodded solemnly and turned away, unable to trust herself to speak. The poor boy had got the words right—as if he had learned a set of phrases—but he was applying them to a finely wrought, sophisticated work that couldn't conceivably be called primitive. She had seen people fall into that trap before.

She guessed people weren't all that different wherever they were—city, country, commuter or hybrid.

And Winston's party wasn't much different from the openings, the avant-garde or retrospective shows that had been such a big part of her father's life. Art to view and to talk about, champagne or highballs, and people gathered together. Mix well and take with an open mind and a grain of salt. She wasn't really disappointed that Winston's party wasn't unique, but she was amused at herself for being so naive that she had expected it to be.

She stood against one of the cedar pillars and sipped her drink, watching Winston's guests drift past. A woman in a peasant blouse covered with hot pink and yellow embroidery went by, propelled by a man in a burnt-orange jump suit. The woman's bracelets jangled as she fanned at the blue cigarette smoke filling the air.

"My God, the fire could be right outside the door and we'd never know it." She let herself be led out the door to the softly lit pool area, not, presumably, to test the air for smoke.

Suddenly materializing from the crowd, Winston leaned over and whispered in her ear, "I want to show you something Dirk brought up from town. The tall boy, with the hair. You've met him?"

She said she'd talked to him, and from what he'd said about the bronze wolf, she knew quite a lot about him. She was trying for a worldly and amused tone, but somehow it came out sounding really catty, and she regretted her words.

"You have him all cataloged and added to the proper list, haven't you, dear?" Winston's eyes were shrewd. "You couldn't be more wrong, but never mind. But do try to remember that people, unlike the paintings and vases you deal with, sometimes refuse to stay where we put them." He patted her arm, adding to her feeling that she'd made far more of a fool of herself than had the pale young man. Winston smiled, as if to show that all was forgiven, and said, "Come along in here, now, and see what Dirk brought me."

He led the way through a wide door into a smaller paneled room. Furnished with several rows of bookcases, a desk and long-necked lamps bowing over suede chairs set on Indian rugs, the room seemed to be a study, or library. Winston crossed to a cabinet as tall as he, of the same light wood as the walls and in the same clean squared-off lines used in the rest of the furnishings in the house. In spite of these similarities, the cabinet looked out of place, and she couldn't think why until Winston unlocked the glass doors across the front. Everything else, Courtney realized—the bronzes, the pre-Columbian heads, the paintings and lithos—were accessible, out where they could be touched and handled. The bookcase was the only thing in the room, perhaps in the whole house, that was locked.

"Isn't this a delight?" Winston gingerly held out a very old-looking book. *The Oregon Trail* was barely visible in gray against a lighter gray cloth cover. "Absolutely mint. Original binding." He looked up at her, searching her face. "You don't understand, do you? I'd have thought you knew something about rare books."

"They always go directly to Mr. Broberg. And he passes them to a rare-book dealer."

"I see. I do realize you need to specialize in your

line of work, my dear. But it doesn't pay to become too narrow, does it?''

She looked up quickly at him. His look seemed to be genuinely sympathetic. A wave of shame washed over her. How dull she must seem to these people, how pedantic and dry. And how arrogant of her to be amused at their superficial knowledge. At least they *had* some knowledge in many fields, while she was as ignorant outside her own specialities as. . .as Floyd.

''Well, that's a pity.'' Winston seemed deflated. ''I do love to share my finds with someone who appreciates them.''

''I'm sorry to disappoint you.''

''Not to worry, my dear. I'm quite used to it. But I warn you, I'll try to convert you. I sometimes think it's my mission in life to try to educate my friends to the glories of rare books.'' He returned the book to the shelf, giving it a final caressing pat as he slid it into place. ''God knows the odds are against success. I even tried to get those Padgett boys to understand. But they weren't interested. More loutish than usual where books were concerned.'' He swept his hand through the air, indicating the bookcase. ''That is one of the finest collections extant on the Oregon Territory.'' He picked up his glass from the table and took a sip. ''What Dirk calls 'Across the Plains with Sunbonnet and Skillet.' '' He giggled. ''But at least he knows that it is a fine collection.''

It took Winston some time to get the door locked with the small key that was attached to a watch chain hanging from his belt. ''I must say I'm surprised at that great gaping hole in your professional knowledge.''

She agreed that she was sadly ignorant, and that seemed to satisfy him. He smiled and once again patted her arm. "And how are you getting along at Rockhurst?"

She told him she was progressing fairly well.

"Have you accomplished what you set out to do?"

Had she? No, not really. The job of cataloging was satisfactory, but she had known she could do that. The success of the sale—the culmination of all these weeks of work—was still an unknown factor. And she hadn't discovered the treasure, and more, she hadn't been able to do a thing to help Sarah. Her eyes met Winston's, and she realized that he too was thinking of the storied, perhaps mythical, treasure. She laughed. "No, I haven't."

"I see." He smiled as if to himself.

Then someone called him from the living room, and with an apologetic bow, he excused himself. She stood beside the bookcase for a moment, thinking about what he'd said. She certainly did have a gaping hole in her learning, and she stared at the books as if they could tell her why they were more valuable than other old books. But they gave her no answers, and as she turned away she saw Daniel in the doorway.

"So this is where you've got to," he said. He started toward her, but Sarah's trilling voice stopped him.

Courtney couldn't hear Sarah's words as she looked up at Daniel, but the woman's voice seemed a little lower, the twitterings slower. She almost leaned against him, and the gray curls at the side of her head, though still in place, were drooping. Courtney guessed she was asking Daniel to get her something, perhaps a tall cool drink. Courtney waved in answer to his smile and helpless shrug, and he took Sarah's elbow, leading her toward the living room.

Poor Sarah, Courtney thought. This crush of hot chattering people was quite a change from the quiet of Rockhurst. Courtney thought she wouldn't be surprised if Sarah were ready to retreat soon—the sooner the better, as far as Courtney was concerned. She was constantly aware of Aaron...always with Samantha nearby. He seemed to be watching Courtney, but she noticed he left the length of the room between them. More than that, he kept between them her fear and suspicion. She had temporarily lost track of him—or he of her—when Winston brought her into the study, but she was all too aware that he was near, out there somewhere in the swirl of partying people.

She had no heart to plunge into the crowd again. She had nothing to say this time around in place of "Doesn't Winston have a lovely house?" She turned back to the quiet of the empty room and wandered around it, gazing, amused at the pieces Winston had chosen to surround himself with in the mountains. She ran her finger along a wooden totem of a bear's head with bared teeth and demonic slanting eyes. She passed by a metal sculpture that she supposed had all sorts of cosmic meaning, but looked to her like a pineapple studded with cheese squares, like the centerpiece at a hotel-catered gallery opening. At the end of the window wall, a sliding door opened onto a small flagstone terrace. Winston was apparently making some attempt to keep his guests from wandering off all over the mountain because all the furniture had been removed, and the only light came from the windows of the room she was in.

She stepped out onto the terrace and breathed the night air deeply, gratefully, of the pine- and fir-scented stillness.

"Nice, isn't it?"

She jumped at the sound of Aaron's voice.

"I'm sorry," he said. "I always seem to be startling you." He was at the edge of the pavement, and as he stepped toward her, the light caught the weary lines of his face. Her heart turned over at the sorrow they seemed to trace.

"It's just...I didn't see you." She backed toward the door. "I didn't mean to barge in."

"Don't go." He stopped where he was. "Unless you don't want to talk to me."

"Nonsense." Irritating man. Why would she avoid talking to him? It was he who had been avoiding her. And now that she was face to face with him, she had no idea what to say. "I was just escaping the crowd, to tell you the truth."

"You too?" There was an odd note in his voice that she couldn't identify. He sounded pleased, almost eager. "The party's going well," he said. "Everyone seems to be having a good time."

"I guess so," she answered, wondering why he cared. "It's hard to tell, at these big parties. But I guess as long as everyone keeps moving and the noise level keeps rising, it's safe to say the party's a big success."

"Well, it's big, anyway. Winston invites everyone from here to Seattle. I don't much like that kind of party."

"Don't you? I love them." Telling herself it wasn't necessary to perjure herself just to be disagreeable, she added, "At least, I like the first hour of a big party. After that there's a sharp decline in my tolerance." Her words embarrassed her. "That wasn't very nice, was it?"

"I don't see anything wrong with it. It was honest." He studied her face for a moment, then said, "While you're in the mood for truth-telling, let me ask you something."

Certain that he was going to confront her with her reaction the day she refused to go with him to find Floyd, she began to turn away, then stopped. After all, this was what she had wanted, wasn't it—a chance to talk to Aaron, to try to undo some of the harm she'd done. She waited wordlessly.

"Look at me," he said. "What do you see?"

What could she tell him? That she saw the man she loved in spite of what he had done or might do? The man she was sorry she had hurt? He wouldn't believe her. Or if he did, he wouldn't want her flawed, imperfect love. She loved him; that was the truth. But there was more—another side. She looked him square in the eye. "I see an overbearing, disagreeable man who is trying to regulate the whole world's behavior."

"Yes, but do you see any bad points?"

She laughed, relieved and delighted that the tension was broken. Again she was surprised by the look in Aaron's eyes. Eagerness, and . . . but it couldn't be a look of yearning. She didn't know what the strange look meant. She only knew it felt good to laugh with him again. "I don't know you, I guess." Suddenly all her notions of who Aaron was and what he was were in doubt.

"No, of course you don't." He sighed, and again she was surprised. "How could you be expected to?" He gave her a small crooked grin and said, "I picked a fine time for a character analysis, didn't I?" He gestured toward the empty terrace. "Let's let the night air and the quiet put us back in shape."

Her heart soared at the prospect of spending a few minutes alone with him, and when he held out his hand to her, her pulse was pounding. They strolled along the terrace and talked about Sarah's pleasure in Winston's party, about Winston's guests, about his house, and Courtney thought she had never known such happiness as she felt just then. In a way, they talked the same small talk she had been making with the strangers in the living room. And yet it was all different. Aaron didn't gloss over the top, seeking fleeting impressions. He delved and seemed to her to find meanings and understanding of people and their doings. As they sat on the low stone wall, she remarked on his ability to see past the trivial, and he denied it.

"I'm not really analytical," he said. "I jump to conclusions, and fall in love at first sight, and leap before I look."

And that left her out, she thought, her happiness vanishing like a star snuffed out. He obviously had not fallen in love with her at first sight. Rather, he had tried his best to get her to leave Rockhurst. "You do all that, do you?" she said in a small defeated voice.

The next thing she knew, Aaron's arms were

around her, and he was kissing her. Longing, desperate kisses at first, that softened and became gentle as she responded warmly. Her head spun and she could hear her blood pounding.

"I love you, Courtney." Before she could answer, he said, "But you're afraid of me, and I don't understand that. I can't handle it."

"It doesn't matter," she said, lifting her face to seek out his kisses again.

"Of course it matters, don't you see that? I can't...." He pushed her from him and stood up. "What are you doing to me? Do you think I'm made of iron?" His voice rasped.

"Aaron...."

"You'd better go in," he said flatly. "They'll be looking for you." He crossed the terrace and slid the glass door open. Standing aside, he barely waited until she crossed the threshold before he pulled the door shut. He hadn't even touched her hand.

Inside, she stood for a moment, bewildered and uncertain. She didn't want to come in—she wanted to be out there with Aaron. But he had sent her away.

Turning, she peered into the darkness of the terrace. Aaron had returned to the wall and stood looking into the depths of the surrounding woods, his face lit by the faint glow from the far window. His fists were clenched at his side. But instead of the square shoulders and angry jutting jaw she was used to, his shoulders were rounded and slumped, his head bent, his chin on his chest.

CHAPTER TEN

AARON APPEARED to have forgotten the meeting on the terrace the moment after it happened. On the way home he was just the same as he had always been, Courtney thought, and there was no sign that those moments had affected him at all.

How different for her. She knew he had said farewell, and she raged silently against the injustice of it. But she knew now just how deeply she had hurt him. He would never forgive her.

After a sleepless night, she resolutely set about banishing Aaron from her thoughts. She told herself she still had a job to do, a job that was becoming more difficult every day. The sensible thing was to concentrate on what she had to do, day by day, starting with this morning. She remembered she had planned something special, different, this morning At last it came to her. She was going to talk to Floyd He was going to tell her what he knew about Jacob's treasure. She hurried to get ready, grateful that she had something important to distract her from her heartache.

As she slipped down the back stairs and out into the yard, she noticed that the sun had already burned the dew from the rhododendrons, and it touched her face with a gentle warmth. In a few hours all the gentleness would be gone, but for the moment it felt good. Her yellow sundress, washed free of the grime it had gathered in the tower, was almost too bright for her eyes in the brittle light. Her low-heeled white shoes made no sound on the red dust, and she realized that the birds, for some reason, were silent. Only the ravens continued their warning caws from some unseen distance, and the only sign of life in the yard was Toby. He came to greet her with his tail wagging and his nose nuzzling under her hand.

In spite of his welcome, she thought Toby seemed somehow worried or unsure of himself. She didn't know—did dogs worry? Or was she being overly sensitive? Perhaps Toby had gotten into some mischief he hoped she hadn't heard about. Or perhaps he was reacting to the strange yellow green cast the sky was taking on as the smoke from the fire drifted west—or to the silence.

Her voice sounded too loud and harsh as she called to Floyd. Quickly she hushed herself and called in a stage whisper, "Floyd?"

She peered into the dark recesses of the barn. The ghostly smell of horses that had been stabled there long ago still permeated the hard-packed earth floor, combined with the smell of today's motor oil and grease.

"Floyd?"

"Shh. Geez, you trying to get them all down here?" Floyd lumbered out of the darkness beyond the big red tractor. "Come on in here where no one'll see you."

Reluctantly, Courtney moved around the tractor. "Everyone's still asleep, I think."

"Not likely. Aaron's probably out at the cut already, and Jenny's up. I seen her out shooing the rabbits a while back." He stood, his feet planted wide apart, and stared at Courtney. She waited, unwilling to do or say anything to frighten him away from giving her whatever information he had, or thought he had. After a long silence, he said, "You didn't make nothing outten that list I gave you?"

"Only that it was book titles," she said. She couldn't really believe the titles had anything to do with Jacob's treasure, but she kept her doubts to herself.

"Well," he said at last, "I was keeping the other half. I kind of. . . I thought maybe it'd be like a secret code, or something, and if I had the other half. . . . I thought it might do me some good."

How could she approach this, she wondered, without scaring him off? "Sometimes, all that sort of thing does is make both halves useless."

"I know that. That's the whole point." He looked disgusted with her. "But then I figured, why give you part of it if I wasn't going to give you the rest." He looked at her defiantly. "I could've kept it all." Then, dropping his gaze to the floor, he added, "But you been nice to me. And I know finding the treasure is part of your job, not just greediness, like it would be for some people around here." He took a deep breath. "So here."

He shoved a piece of paper across to her. It was crumpled and worn, like the other piece he had left her. And it had one torn edge that looked as if it would match perfectly the edge of the list of book titles. She had no doubt they were part of the same paper. Floyd waited expectantly. "Well?"

She shook her head. "I still don't know anything." It was a list of dates and cities, again in Jacob's handwriting. "I'll have to compare the two halves to see what it means." But in the back of her mind there was a tiny tingle of excitement. She knew one thing the dates might mean. But she was far from certain, and it was too soon to tell Floyd and arouse his expectations. "May I keep this?"

He glared at her for a moment. "Just don't forget where you got it."

That reminded her of the reason Floyd was so sure the list was important. "Where did you get it?"

He gave her the sheepish grin that said he knew he'd done something he shouldn't have. "Found it under the blotter on his desk. After he died."

Her fingers curled around the paper convulsively. It was stolen information, something she had no right to. She began to protest, then hesitated. If she turned the list over to the family, to whom it rightly belonged, who would see to it that Sarah got her share of the proceeds? Who would see that she got any? Courtney decided to keep the list to herself, at least until she could decide what was the right thing to do. Promising to remember her benefactor, she escaped from the barn as quickly as she could.

Back in her room, she got the other list from the bottom of her dresser drawer and spread the two pieces of paper out side by side on the bed. She matched up the rough, torn edges. Now the entries were complete:

Vanity Fair   William Makepeace Thackeray
London, 1848
A Tale of Two Cities   Charles Dickens
London, 1859

There were several more. The dates were all early, probably the dates the books were published. The tingle inside her grew. First editions? If Jacob had discovered their current value shortly before his death, then surely he would have been surprised and elated.

Was it possible that a dedicated collector hadn' known of the tremendous leaps in value that books had taken within the last ten years? Even she, as uninformed as she was, knew that. But of course it was possible, she told herself. Jacob was less interested in value, really, than in accumulation for its own sake. Then too, the book world and the art world barely touched one another, only overlapping in a few specialized areas. Hadn't Winston Coe told her just last night—could the party have been only last night?—that she was an ignorant girl because she hadn't recognized the value of his newest Oregon Territory acquisition?

Suddenly she wondered if Winston had shown her the book not so much because he was proud of it, but to see if she knew about books. Because Winston must have known about Jacob's first editions. They had talked together over the years, and Jacob had consulted Winston. Suddenly, she was convinced that there were first editions, and that Winston knew about them. Was he just playing games with them—pushing her, a pawn, one square forward, pushing

Sarah, a queen, two squares to the side—to see what would happen, to amuse himself? Did he know where they were, and did he prefer to wait instead of telling them, to see how long it took to find them? Or was there an even more sinister explanation? Did he hope to buy up the books at trash prices and realize a profit from his friends' ignorance?

She stared, unseeing, at the list; then gradually one characteristic caught her attention. They were all such familiar titles. Freshman classics, most of them. Were they hidden in plain sight, like Poe's purloined letter? So familiar that the eye passed right over them?

With a rush of excitement, she pushed the papers into her skirt pocket and hurried out into the hall. She ran lightly, quickly down the stairs. This time she was grateful for the sound-swallowing effect of the high ceilings and deep carpets. At the foot of the stairs, she stopped and listened. There seemed to be no one around. She closed the library doors quietly behind her and stood looking the room over, much as she had on that first day at Rockhurst.

The huge desk, the gilded lamps, the black and empty fireplace told her nothing. On both sides of the fireplace the bookshelves had been torn out to make room for the jade cabinet and shelves of cloisonné and porcelain. But on the east wall, opposite the fireplace, were floor-to-ceiling shelves filled with books faded from the afternoon sun—sun that Jacob wouldn't allow to fall on his art treasures.

She went closer to read the titles. A ten-volume set of *The Wit and Humor of America,* circa 1920; some Kathleen Norris and Edna Ferber novels, all of them in frayed bindings as if Jacob had bought them in a job lot from a sidewalk used-book bin. An old set of encyclopedias with the G-H volume missing. The Graustark novels in cheap editions. A motley collection of books on logging, mechanics, law and health. None of them was worth more than fifty cents.

She pulled out volume after volume to look at those that had been pushed behind. Every title had to be read; this was no time for skimming. She was conscious of time passing and an unexplained feeling that she must hurry. Still, she had to be thorough. She was more and more convinced that the first editions existed. They were as real to her now as if she had seen them herself.

She wondered again if Winston knew where Jacob had hidden them and why he hadn't told Sarah about them. She realized that not only were the books real to her, but so was Winston's knowledge of them. She decided she had to see him as soon as she could. She didn't think he would tell her what he knew, but she felt confident that she could get confirmation of her strong feelings that there were valuable books somewhere at Rockhurst—and perhaps confirmation that Winston knew where they were.

She saw with dismay that it was almost time for Rockhurst's big midday Sunday meal. Although last night's party had caused breakfast to be taken off the schedule, Courtney was sure there would be a full table at dinner. Sarah would want to talk about the party—the guests, what they wore, what they said—and relive her pleasure, and she would want everyone there to talk about it too. But if she hurried, Courtney still had time to run over to Winston's and be back before Jenny called them all to dinner. She had wasted valuable time in the library, but she wouldn't let another moment get away. And she didn't want to stop when Floyd stepped out of the shadows on the second-floor landing and said, "Well?"

"Listen, Floyd, I'm in an awful hurry. I haven't discovered anything on my own, but I'm going over to Winston Coe's. I think he can help us."

Floyd was not at all in favor of bringing Winston into the search, but when she insisted, he grudgingly agreed. "But I don't want everybody in the place to know about that list. I could get into trouble. Don't you tell him where you got it."

"I don't think I'll even mention that there is a list," Courtney assured him. She promised to be as close-mouthed as he himself had been. That seemed to please him, and he grinned as she hurried on to her room to get her car keys.

THE KEYS WEREN'T IN HER PURSE. Her jacket and coat pockets were empty. This was ridiculous, she thought, and of course it had to happen when she was in a hurry. She opened the dresser drawers and rummaged through the few things she had brought with her from Seattle; still she couldn't find the keys. She went back to her purse and dumped it out on the bed. She found old shopping lists and a wad of Kleenex and a lipstick she thought she'd lost, but no keys. Irritated, she slammed everything back into the purse and tossed it onto the bed. She had never left her keys in the car before in her life, but she supposed there was a first time for everything. Convinced that love and Rockhurst and Jacob's treasure had combined to turn her brain to mush, she hurried back down the stairs and out into the heat.

Under a sky that was growing gray and yellow like a nasty bruise, her car sat patiently, ready to do her bidding. But without any keys. She pulled open the door and leaned in to confirm what she had already seen. There were no keys in the ignition.

But there was a large cardboard carton in the back. Even before she pulled up the flaps, she knew what she would find. It was a carton of books. Somehow, she wasn't even surprised. It was almost as if she had been expecting to find them here. Perhaps it was merely because her keys had been missing. Or was it because her job here was almost finished, and the sale would be held soon, meaning that everything in the house would be turned over and examined and later carried away? It was because the sale was drawing near that Floyd had been prompted to give her the other half of the list. And now it had prompted someone to move the books. She knelt on the front seat, leaning over the headrest to pull out one of the books: *A Tale of Two Cities*. She realized now that the familiarity she had felt with those titles on Jacob's list was more than just a memory from English Lit I. She had actually seen these books—recently—in the tower. The cartons of books that she had assumed had been taken from the library to make room for the jade cabinet.

That may have been exactly what had happened, and may have been the moment Jacob found out they had some value. Flipping to the title page, she checked the date: 1859. She didn't remember if that was the publishing date on the list, but it was early enough so that it probably was.

Turning around in the seat, she sat with the book in her hand, staring at it as if it would tell her how the carton got in her car and who put it there.

"Hello, pretty lady." Daniel dropped his voice as he leaned in the doorway. "I see you found the books."

Relief flooded through her that it was Daniel who had lugged the books down here. He would be able to help her decide how to handle them.

"You know what I think those are?" He looked around as if checking to see if they were alone. "Scrunch over and I'll tell you something that'll set your pretty little head spinning. I don't want...the wrong people to hear."

She supposed he meant Aaron, and she was heartsick that Aaron would be the one to plot against Sarah. She scrambled with some difficulty from one bucket seat to the other, letting Daniel into the driver's side.

Again he looked over his shoulder. He pulled her keys from his shirt pocket. "I found these on the hall floor and I figured they were yours." While he was talking, he started the engine, turned the car around in the spacious yard and started down the drive. "I think we might even be better off out of the yard altogether. Whatta you think?"

What she thought was that he was getting carried away with his precautions. Still, he'd always been the calm serene one, so perhaps all this secrecy was necessary. "Where are we going?"

"Just for a ride. To talk a little bit." He darted a glance sideways at her, and she saw how sober and intense he looked, not at all like his usual self.

"About those books. I saw them in the tower about a year ago. And I got a hunch. I mean, why would Jacob have them up there, separate from the other junk in the attic?" He tapped his forehead. "So I put the old noggin to work."

As they turned onto the county road and headed up the mountain, he flashed her a grin. For the first time since she'd known him, his smile looked false. And as if part of the same thought, she realized he couldn't have found her keys in the hallway. Her eyes opened wide. She had been up and down those stairs a dozen times this morning, and if he'd found them earlier, why hadn't he returned them?

"I saw you talking to Winston," Daniel said, "and looking at his old books last night. I knew you were onto the treasure." He was pushing the VW faster than Courtney knew it should go. His smile had faded. "Old Winston's always trying to educate someone about what to look for and all that."

"Are we going to see him now? To ask him about the chance of the books being valuable?" She grasped at the possibility. "Because that's just what I was going to do."

"Were you, now? Well, I suppose we could do that. Or we could have. But old Winston's gone. He and Samantha stopped by about an hour ago to say that they and all their house guests have left. Because of the fire. Spent the whole morning packing up everything and took off."

They must have come by while she was in the library, she thought. Or upstairs vainly searching for her keys.

"Samantha wanted Aaron to leave with them."

Courtney's heart lurched.

Daniel's laugh was cruel. "I used to think I had a chance with you, when you first came. But it didn't take you long to fall for the Avenging Angel, did it? Well, you might have lost him to the beautiful Samantha. I don't doubt he would have gone with her. But he wasn't around when they came by. He was doing another good deed, taking the tractor down to the ranger station for the fire fighters to use." Blandly he added, "I wonder if he'll get back safely."

She stared at him, horrified. How could she not have seen this monster hiding behind Daniel's grin? "Have you done anything to the tractor?"

"Of course not." He sounded scandalized. Then a half-smile appeared on his lips. "I didn't have to. My guess is the fire's going to take care of anyone left up here in a couple of hours. Even if he borrows a car to get back to the house, it'll be cutting it pretty close."

"And where will you be?"

"I'll be long gone."

"With the books."

"Of course with the books. That's what this is all about. And anyone who's interested will think the Ol' Fire got me, too."

The truth hit her with full force then—Daniel meant every word he was saying. Desperately, she tried to think of some way to stop him. She tried another tactic. "How do you know the books are valuable? They could be just what they look like. Old used books."

"You forget—Winston set out to teach Aaron and me about rare books once. And I took in a lot more than either of them thought I did. I know what to look for. And just to make certain, I checked with a dealer in San Francisco. The same one I sold the first couple of books to." He laughed. "You didn't know that, did you?"

"Have you taken other pieces, too?"

"Not much." He pouted. "Most of it's on that stupid inventory the lawyer made out for probating the will. He didn't know what anything was worth, but he knew enough to list it anyway."

And that, she supposed, had stopped Daniel from siphoning off many of the smaller pieces. Nervously, she ran her tongue over her dry lips. "What are you going to do now?" What was he going to do with her, she meant.

"Just take you up the mountain a little way. About fifteen, twenty miles, maybe."

She frowned, puzzled.

"Well, my dear, I don't want your blood on my hands. I don't want a body found with marks all over it, as if there'd been foul play, now do I? I mean, if it's going to look as if I perished in the fire, we can't have any suspicions aroused. Nobody saw you leave Rockhurst with me."

She remembered the many times she'd thought how easily people could come and go there without anyone else seeing them. That was why she had been afraid to go with Aaron to get Floyd—because no one had seen her leave the house. Her heart was heavy at the waste, the heartache she had caused.

Daniel took the car around a sharp curve, sliding perilously close to the rocky edge of the road. Courtney looked down over the steep drop onto wisps of smoke caught in the tops of fir trees far below them.

With the car under control again, Daniel said, "I'm letting nature take its course. You learn to trust nature up here in the woods. They may or may not be able to identify your bones—if they find them. Either way, there'll be nothing to connect you with me."

"That's ridiculous. The fire might not even come this way."

"It will." He seemed certain. "There's a draw about fifteen miles up, where the wind comes through. That's the path it'll take." He spoke in a conversational tone, as if he were discussing where to start cutting next spring. She shivered.

They had passed the logging road leading to Winston's house and were in an area new to her. The sky was darkening with billowing gray clouds of smoke. The trees grew darker as the light dimmed, their limbs more menacing. Like the trees outside the room where the icons were kept, near the tower.

"Did you turn on the gas in the tower?" she asked suddenly.

"Well, that was a mistake," he answered plaintively.

"You weren't trying to kill me?"

"Of course I was. But it was a mistake, because I thought you had seen the books and gone back up there to check them out. I mean, you're the art expert. I thought for sure you'd know what they were worth. But you didn't, did you?"

She shook her head, then muttered, "No."

"Yeah. Well, when you didn't mention them, and nothing else happened after the big do-gooder saved you, I realized you had passed them by, the same as everyone else." He laughed shortly. "For a while I thought you never would put two and two together.'' He turned his head to look at her. "I really hoped that was the way it would be.''

While Courtney was trying desperately to think what she should do, Daniel seemed to be following his own train of thought. "I'm going to get more for these books than the measly third I'd get from your sale.''

Courtney thought he was wrong. Everyone at Rockhurst underrated Jacob's collection. But she wasn't interested in what he believed. "What are you going to do...after you dump me?''

He hesitated for a moment, as if he hadn't quite decided, then said, "The best thing would be to smash your car and leave it there. That would explain what you're doing so far from the house. But of course, I've got to get out. With the tractor gone and the pickup as usual not working, I've got to have it.''

He was leaving the station wagon for the others. As if he could read her thoughts, he said, "Well, what kind of a monster do you think I am? I couldn't just leave them all without some way to get away. As long as they don't suspect me of anything, I've got nothing against them.''

They were still speeding up the mountain, and Courtney realized that the farther they went, the poorer her chances were of escaping. She looked across at him; he was bent slightly over the steering wheel, smiling and darting quick wary glances at her as he maneuvered the car around the turns at breakneck speed. Where was the casual, easygoing Daniel she had known all these weeks? "I always thought you were the relaxed one at Rockhurst," she said.

"So did everyone else, sweetie. So did everyone else." He laughed harshly to himself. "And that made them relax, too, you see."

They came to a short stretch of straight roadway, and Daniel's grip on the wheel loosened a fraction. The speed at which he was driving required constant attention to the twisting road, but she felt the lessening of tension. He began to expand on his role at Rockhurst, complaining that Aaron had all the responsibilities—and the authority. He talked about Jacob's always promising Aaron a bigger part of the business.

While he talked, going over his grievances, Courtney watched the road. It had climbed past the sheer drop, and now they were crossing a boulder-strewn meadow between low rises covered with salal and bear-berry and the dried remnants of summer flowers. A few snaggle-toothed firs reared up in the alien ground. Just ahead a rolling hill dropped to a stream surrounded by brush and low alder saplings.

In this beautiful harsh countryside, he was driving her to her death. In a strange lucid moment, she considered this without any panic or emotion. Was she going to let him do that without even putting up some sort of struggle? A line came to her from the hundreds of gangster movies she'd seen on TV. *Well,* she quoted to herself, *if I'm going, I'm not going alone.* She would crash the car, with both of them in it before she'd let him kill her like a docile sheep.

She reached her foot over and jammed it down on top of his on the gas pedal. They shot forward. Cursing, he pushed her off and kicked her foot away. She grabbed the steering wheel and gave it a wrench.

They swerved to the edge of the road, almost side-swiping a huge boulder. He pulled the car back, and again she tried for the gas pedal.

"Damn it, you trying to get us both killed?" he shouted.

"Yes. We'll die together."

"My God, you're crazy!" Slowing the car down a fraction, he reached over and pulled open her door handle. He tried to push her out. She fought back, grabbing for the steering wheel. He was going to throw her onto one of the boulders that edged the road, unless she could time it to fall where the shoulder was flat and cushioned with wild grasses. Daniel put his left foot on the gas pedal and turned to push her out the door with his other foot. The car, still racing along the road, lost speed as he made the move. At that instant, Courtney jumped.

Her shoulder hit the gravel, and she tumbled onto the bed of earth and weeds. She kept her arms and legs pulled up around her body and let herself roll. When she stopped, she knew she had rolled all the way down the hill. The sound of water was close by. She heard Daniel calling from the road, and he sounded gratifyingly far away.

She let her arms and legs fall free, sprawled out against the dark brown earth. She knew that even in the smoky dusk, her bright yellow dress was visible for a good distance. She thought of pretending to be hurt. But he might just carry her back to the car. Or she could run. But she would lose to him in a flight through these rough woods. Her only hope was to feign unconsciousness. It was a poor defense, but she had no time to think further. She heard him coming closer. She steeled herself to stay very still.

"Courtney? Now, that was a very foolish thing to do, little lamb. You could have hurt yourself. Courtney?"

She dared not breathe.

"Damn." A twig snapped up the hill as Daniel evidently tripped or turned his ankle. "Come on, Courtney. Let's quit horsing around now. Let's get out of here." Again he faltered on the treacherous terrain. He was so close now, she could hear his footsteps on the dried twigs. He cursed again as he scrambled across a rocky patch. She didn't move.

"Courtney?" He had stopped. "Courtney, you all right?" There was a long silence. "Are you playing possum, Courtney? Because you know what they do with possums, don't you, honey. They put a bullet through their heads. Just to make sure. That what you want?" He took another step, stumbled, cursed and stopped. She could feel his eyes boring into her.

A sudden breeze blew up, sending needles and fallen alder leaves drifting across her face. With it came a strong odor of smoke. She couldn't see what Daniel was doing, but there seemed to be a suspension of movement, and she imagined him lifting his head and sniffing the smoke-laden air

"I got to get out of here," he muttered. There was another second's silence, then he said, "I reckon you'll do." He spoke so softly, she could hardly hear. Evidently he was talking to himself. "If you do come to before the fire gets here, you've got too far to walk to make it out. Everybody'll be long gone from the mountain." Another eternity, then, "Too bad, pretty lady. But you should have stuck to your job and not gone treasure hunting." He laughed. "That's for pirates."

She heard him struggling back up the hill. After a while, she heard the car start. Still she dared not take so much as a deep breath. She knew Daniel was clever enough to keep watching her for as long as he could. She bitterly regretted the bright yellow dress. She heard the car turn around and start back down the mountain. She waited until the sound of the engine disappeared down the curving road. At last certain she was out of Daniel's sight, she began to try to move. She had no idea whether she was badly hurt; she knew shock would mask the pain for a while if she was. The first impact on the gravel had been bad, but the buffeting down the hill had been cushioned by the inches-deep bed of dry grass. She hoped it had done its job.

CHAPTER ELEVEN

AS AARON TURNED IN under the wooden arch and began the twisting drive to Rockhurst, the sound of a VW engine high in the mountains above him was less than an echo. Lost in the noise of the old Dodge truck he had borrowed at the ranger station, the sound passed over him. His thoughts were on getting the family out of the house and down off the mountain.

There was no one in the hall, but a call brought an answering yodel from Sarah's room. He found Sarah and Jenny arguing over the clothes laid out on Sarah's bed.

"You ain't gonna need all them clothes. You better hurry, instead of trying to take everything you own," Jenny said.

"But we don't know how long we'll have to be gone," Sarah objected.

"You'd think this was some kind of game or something. Oh, there you are," Jenny said as Aaron came in. "Tell her this isn't a vacation, will you?"

"Jenny's right," he said. "Just take what you have to. Where's Courtney?" he asked, ignoring Sarah's protests.

"She must have left with Daniel," Jenny said. "Her car's gone, and I haven't seen either of them all morning."

With her head bent over the suitcase, Sarah watched Aaron from the corner of her eye. "I must say, I'm surprised at her, walking off without a word."

"Maybe she was scared," Jenny said. She, too, looked sideways at Aaron. "People get scared, you know," she said gently, as if explaining something to him.

"I know." He patted her hand. "At least she's safe from the fire." He took a deep breath. "Let's get on with it. We've got to leave as soon as you're packed."

"Radio said the fire's crossed the summit and is headed this way," Jenny said.

"And Winston came by," Sarah said, "and he and all his guests were evacuating. He said we'd better do the same." Her eyes glittered with excitement. "But fire or no fire, I must have something to wear."

"Yes, of course, but you've got to hurry." While Aaron helped Jenny bring an armful of clothes from the closet, Sarah quickly pushed a Dresden dancer and a fan from the wall into the suitcase. Aaron dropped the clothes on the bed beside some official-looking papers in an open black leather document case. "What's all this? Do you need these? They look like something that should have been in a safe-deposit box."

Sarah gave a short laugh. "They were far safer with me." She snatched at them, but Aaron already had one of them in his hand. He held it up and read it. "Ah, yes," he said with a smile.

Sarah stared at him. "You don't sound surprised."

"At what?" Jenny asked, coming to peer around his shoulder to read the paper. "That's a marriage license."

It was made out for Anabelle Padgett and John Tuttle, King County, State of Washington. Duly signed and witnessed.

"She was married?" Jenny's voice went up. "And you never said anything?"

Sarah began to protest, but Aaron interrupted her. He had known for years, he said, and trusted that she had had good reason for concealing his legitimate birth. It hadn't seemed important to him by the time he found out the truth.

"I thought it had started as a way of protecting my mother."

"Yes, yes, that's right," Sarah said eagerly. "You know Jacob was bad enough, thinking she'd just run off. But if he'd known she was really married, he'd have...it's hard to explain, but I think—we both thought—that he'd have figured he didn't own her any more. We were afraid he'd throw her out. And she wasn't strong, you know."

"I know."

"Then, after she died...."

"You were afraid to tell him what you'd done."

Sarah nodded, looking relieved that he seemed to understand. Then she cocked her head. "But you knew about it? All the time he was abusing you, calling you names, you knew, and you didn't give me away?" Sarah's thin hands fluttered at her breast. "I think you did that to protect me," she said wonderingly. "But why?"

Jenny snorted. "You're a bigger fool than I

thought you was, Sarah Padgett. Why do you think he stayed here all these years?''

Sarah turned to stare at her. ''Why to protect his inheritance. To work the land.''

''That's right,'' Aaron said quickly, stuffing the papers in among Sarah's clothes in the suitcase. ''Log the timber and run the business.''

''Hah!'' Jenny snorted again. ''To look after you, you fool woman.''

Sarah continued to stare at Aaron.

''Because he loves you, you old fool,'' Jenny said.

''I wish you'd told me,'' Sarah said at last. ''All those years,'' she sighed.

''I never was good at expressing my feelings,'' Aaron said.

''Ask me, you'd better learn,'' Jenny advised.

''What we'd all better do is get ready.'' He shut the suitcase and snapped the latches. ''I'll put this in the station wagon. Jenny, get your things together. The absolute minimum, remember.'' He turned back to Sarah. ''Now, this is all you can take. No more.''

Sarah looked pained as she watched him leave. ''Give me the keys, please,'' she said to Jenny when Aaron was gone. She stood with her hand outstretched, obviously expecting obedience.

Full of objections, Jenny at last gave in and unhooked the household keys from her waist. Glaring at Sarah, she turned and stomped out of the room. Sarah went to the door and watched until Jenny was out of sight. Then, fishing a rumpled piece of paper from her dress pocket, she looked it over and, moving quickly, walked over to the stairs and up to the third floor.

AARON OPENED THE TAILGATE of the Chevy wagon and tossed Sarah's suitcase in. As he turned away, Floyd came across the yard.

"We going soon?" he asked.

Aaron said they would leave as soon as the women were ready. "There'll be Sarah, Jenny, you and me."

"What about Miss Courtney?" Floyd asked. "Ain't we waiting for her?"

"She's gone. She left with Daniel this morning."

"Oh. Okay." Floyd lumbered back toward the barn.

When Aaron was almost at the back door, Floyd called to him. "No, she didn't." He shuffled on across the yard.

Aaron stopped, his blood turning cold. "Floyd. Come here. What do mean, 'No, she didn't.'" He ran across the red dust toward Floyd, who stood and watched. "She didn't leave with Daniel?"

"I don't know nothing about what Daniel did." Floyd blinked at him.

"About Courtney. What about her?"

"She didn't leave this morning. I seen her."

"When?"

"I don't know." Floyd squirmed under the intensity of Aaron's questions "Sometime. But it was close to noon."

"Where? Where is she now? What did she say?" Aaron tried to slow his words down. He could see he was frightening Floyd, but he wanted to grab him and shake the information out of him. "Now, just take it easy and tell me what she said."

"Take it easy yourself," Floyd said sulkily. "She said she was going over to Winston Coe's."

"But he's left."

"Well, we didn't know that then. And I know she wasn't with him when he came by here. Only him and that snooty girl, Jenny said."

Aaron had already started toward the front of the house. "Tell the women I'll be back." At the corner of the house, he stopped and called back, "If I'm not back in an hour, Floyd, leave. Take the others in the station wagon and get out. Understand?"

Aaron ran to the front of the house and jumped in the old Dodge truck he had borrowed to get home. It responded quickly, and he spun onto the drive, spraying gravel. On the county road, Aaron pushed the accelerator hard, making the old truck quiver and shake in protest. As he drove, he tried to figure how long Courtney had been gone from Rockhurst. But he had nothing to go on. All Floyd knew was she had been there sometime around noon. An hour ago. Why would she go to Winston's? Why hadn't she seen him when he came by the house? Aaron didn't even know if she had driven—or if Daniel had her car and she had walked. His heart quailed at the thought. He prayed she hadn't walked. If she was cutting through the woods, he would never find her in time. He swung the truck off the county road and onto the old logging road.

The very air around Winston's house had an abandoned feel, and the house was obviously deserted. Aaron jumped out of the truck and ran to the front door. He rang the bell and pounded on the door, but the hollow echo told him no one was there. Back in the truck he turned it around, bumping up over the garden, and headed back down the logging road.

Quickly, he went over the possibilities. He hadn't passed Courtney on the way up. She wasn't familiar with the country; had she missed Winston's road and gone farther up the mountain? Or was she cutting through the woods on foot? He cast a hasty glance at the darkening sky. An unnatural dusk had turned the afternoon to a somber twilight. At the county road, he turned uphill.

COURTNEY HEARD THE SOUND of an engine coming closer and tried to hurry across the bumpy ground. It was getting so dark she couldn't see well. Her ankle hurt worse with each step, and she leaned hard on the long stick she was using as a crutch. She had to get to the road in time to stop that car. Her brow was wet from the pain, and she felt chilled in spite of the warm wind that scattered bits of ash like blackened snowflakes. The smoke in the air was making her cough.

She heard the brakes screech and looked up to see an old truck stop at the edge of the road. Then, unbelievably, Aaron was running across the field to her. She wondered if she was hallucinating. But his hard strong arms were real as they crushed her to him.

"What happened? Are you all right? Oh, God, I've been so worried." In a shower of love, his kisses washed away the memory of fear and suspicion, the hurt she had caused. He had forgotten, or forgiven her, and that was all she needed to know. He kissed her forehead, her cheeks, her eyes. "How is it your face is always dirty?" he murmured against her cheek. Then, holding her by the shoulders, he looked at her. "What are you doing out here?"

Briefly, she told him about Daniel and the books. He made no comment except to say, ''Thank God you're all right.''

Again he kissed her lips. She melted against him, and their bodies were as one. His strong arms supported her. His love washed over her like a warm wave.

THEY HURRIED UP the front steps of Rockhurst and found Floyd and Jenny at the foot of the great staircase. Over and over Floyd moaned, ''What are we going to do?'' Jenny was kneeling at the foot of the stairs, crying. Beside her, lying in a crumpled heap, was Sarah. Courtney felt as if she had lived through this whole scene before, but like a sudden freezing blast, she knew this time it was different. Aaron crossed the hall in two strides and dropped to his knees beside Sarah. A few quick movements, a fingertip at her throat, and then he was perfectly still.

Courtney knew without asking that Sarah was dead.

At her feet was a large suitcase, the latches broken from the fall, the contents spilling out over the flowered carpet. There was the pink jade Buddha, the celery-colored jade bowl, and the bird that Courtney had examined the day she arrived. Her mind flashed back to that day, and her pleasure at finding such a good collection of jade. Among the folds of the teal blue dress, she could see the edges of an icon. The three saints. From the way the dress draped, Courtney could tell that the others were there also. Sarah seemed to have gone unerringly to the best, most valuable pieces, Courtney thought with surprise. She had thought that Sarah had no idea of the relative values of Jacob's possessions.

"Look at this," Jenny said, her voice thick with grief. "She had this in her hand, the damned fool." She shoved a small piece of paper at Aaron.

He looked at it, frowning, and handed it to Courtney. "Yours?"

It was the missing page from Courtney's notebook—the page that listed the most valuable pieces. "Yes," she said in a small voice. She didn't want to tell Aaron where the list came from.

But he seemed to know. "I suppose she took this from your desk?"

Courtney nodded.

"Why didn't you tell me? No, never mind, I know the answer. You thought I had taken it."

Courtney could say nothing.

"Never mind, my dearest, I understand. How could you know?" He turned back to gaze at Sarah's lifeless body. "Poor Sarah. Her greed got her, after all. That was what kept her at Rockhurst when she could have—should have—escaped. And now...."

"Now she has escaped," Jenny said. "And she must have died happy, thinking about how she was getting away at last."

Aaron picked up the tiny body and stood up. "We'll take her down the mountain."

WITH SARAH LYING in the back of the station wagon, a blanket pulled up over her sightless eyes, they were at last ready to leave. Aaron rolled up the windows to shut out the drifting ashes, and was about to start the engine when Jenny said, "Hear that roar?"

For an instant they all listened to the rumble. "That's the fire," she said. "Will the house make it through, do you think?"

Before he answered, Aaron looked for a moment at the house. Then he shook his head. "It's not likely. The rangers don't have much hope of saving anything above Harrington's."

"All that stuff," Jenny said from the back seat. "All them pots and vases. They'll all burn up."

"There's no help for it," Aaron said. "And I don't feel any sense of loss." He started the engine. "Whatever Jacob felt about his collection, it never brought anything but pain to anyone else." He turned to gaze at Courtney. "That's why I wanted you to leave. From the very first, I was afraid you'd be hurt." His eyes hardened. "And if I'd known how dangerous it really was for you, I'd have got you out of here."

Courtney reached over and took his hand. "Never mind, it's all over now. Daniel didn't hurt me." She looked at him. "But he did get away with Jacob's secret treasure.'

"Well, I can't forgive him for what he tried to do to you," Aaron said. "But I'm glad he's got the books. Rockhurst owed him something. Maybe if things had been more fair, he wouldn't have done what he did." He smiled at her. "They can't take the important things from me."

"The land?"

He laughed. "The land," he agreed. "But most important—you."

He leaned across to kiss her, oblivious to the smiles and nudges of Jenny and Floyd behind them in the back seat. Then he released her and turned to open his door. He leaned out and whistled. "Toby. Here, Toby."

"You ain't letting that smelly dog in here, are you?" Jenny complained.

Beside her, Floyd guffawed. "He don't like riding."

"You want me to leave him here in the fire?"

"No, 'course not," Jenny conceded.

Reluctantly, the dog obeyed Aaron's command to get in front and sit at Courtney's feet. He curled up there, unhappy, but trusting things would work out for the best, as the station wagon started down the long twisting drive.

A pair of ravens flew up from a cedar beside the road, startled by the car's approach. Courtney remembered that she had seen ravens the day she arrived at Rockhurst, and she had thought them mournful birds. Scavengers, Jenny said. Like the Padgetts, they waited to grab what they could. The forest was quiet now—all the other creatures had fled the danger long ago. Only the ravens remained. Waiting.

They drove some distance in silence, then Jenny gasped, "Oh, my God."

Courtney turned and saw Jenny staring openmouthed at the house. Courtney's heart leaped in fear and sorrow as she saw through the veil of trees that a flying spark had found the tower already. Flames were spreading down the tower walls and reaching for the main roof.

As the trees shut off her view momentarily, Courtney thought, as Jenny had, of the artwork, the inlaid floors, and the grand staircase—all lost. But perhaps, too, the fire would purge Rockhurst of Jacob's evil spirit. The land was good; some of the trees would survive, and others could be replanted. Together, she and Aaron would make a new Rockhurst, a Rockhurst built on love. She thought of all the years Aaron had held onto the belief that some day he would find love, and someone to love him.

She reached over and put her hand on his. "I'll never stop telling you," she said, "I love you."

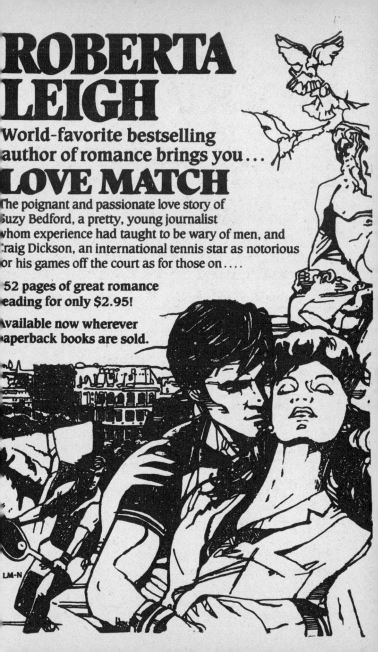

ROBERTA LEIGH

A specially designed collection of six exciting love stories by one of the world's favorite romance writers—Roberta Leigh, author of more than 60 bestselling novels!

1 Love in Store   4 The Savage Aristocrat
2 Night of Love   5 The Facts of Love
3 Flower of the Desert   6 Too Young to Love

Available in August wherever paperback books are sold, or available through Harlequin Reader Service. Simply complete and mail the coupon below.

Harlequin Reader Service

In the U.S.
P.O. Box 52040
Phoenix, AZ 85072-9988

In Canada
649 Ontario Street
Stratford, Ontario N5A 6W2

Please send me the following editions of the Harlequin Roberta Leigh Collector's Editions. I am enclosing my check or money order for $1.95 for each copy ordered, plus 75¢ to cover postage and handling.

☐ 1   ☐ 2   ☐ 3   ☐ 4   ☐ 5   ☐ 6

Number of books checked_____ @ $1.95 each = $_____

N.Y. state and Ariz. residents add appropriate sales tax $_____

Postage and handling $___.75___

TOTAL $_____

I enclose_____

(Please send check or money order. We cannot be responsible for cash sent through the mail.) Price subject to change without notice.

NAME_____
(Please Print)
ADDRESS_____ APT. NO._____

CITY_____

STATE/PROV._____ ZIP/POSTAL CODE_____

Offer expires January 31, 1984   30756000000

1. How do you rate _____ ?

(Please print book TITLE)

1.6 ☐ excellent   .4 ☐ good   .2 ☐ not so good
.5 ☐ very good   .3 ☐ fair   .1 ☐ poor

2. How likely are you to purchase another book in this series?
2.1 ☐ definitely would purchase   .3 ☐ probably would not purchase
.2 ☐ probably would purchase   .4 ☐ definitely would not purchase

3. How do you compare this book with similar books you usually read?
3.1 ☐ far better than others   .4 ☐ not as good
.2 ☐ better than others   .5 ☐ definitely not as good
.3 ☐ about the same

4. Have you any additional comments about this book?

_____ (4)

_____ (6)

5. How did you *first* become aware of this book?
8. ☐ read other books in series   11. ☐ friend's recommendation
9. ☐ in-store display   12. ☐ ad inside other books
10. ☐ TV, radio or magazine ad   13. ☐ other _____

(please specify)

6. What *most* prompted you to buy this book?
14. ☐ read other books in series   17. ☐ title   20. ☐ story outline on back
15. ☐ friend's recommendation   18. ☐ author   21. ☐ read a few pages
16. ☐ picture on cover   19. ☐ advertising   22. ☐ other _____

(please specify)

J12

7. What type(s) of paperback fiction have you purchased in the past 3 months? Approximately how many?

	No. purchased		No. purchased
☐ contemporary romance	(23) ____	☐ espionage	(37) ____
☐ historical romance	(25) ____	☐ western	(39) ____
☐ gothic romance	(27) ____	☐ contemporary novels	(41) ____
☐ romantic suspense	(29) ____	☐ historical novels	(43) ____
☐ mystery	(31) ____	☐ science fiction/fantasy	(45) ____
☐ private eye	(33) ____	☐ occult	(47) ____
☐ action/adventure	(35) ____	☐ other	(49) ____

8. Have you purchased any books from any of these series in the past 3 months? Approximately how many?

	No. purchased		No. purchased
☐ Harlequin Romance	(51) ____	☐ Harlequin American Romance	(55) ____
☐ Harlequin Presents	(53) ____	☐ Superromance	(57) ____

9. On which date was this book purchased? (59) _____

10. Please indicate your age group and sex.
61.1 ☐ Male   62.1 ☐ under 15   .3 ☐ 25-34   .5 ☐ 50-64
.2 ☐ Female   .2 ☐ 15-24   .4 ☐ 35-49   .6 ☐ 65 or older

PRINTED IN CANADA

Thank you for completing and returning this questionnaire.

NAME _____
(Please Print)

ADDRESS _____

CITY _____

ZIP CODE _____

BUSINESS REPLY MAIL

FIRST CLASS   **PERMIT NO. 70**   **TEMPE, AZ.**

POSTAGE WILL BE PAID BY ADDRESSEE

NATIONAL READER SURVEYS

1440 SOUTH PRIEST DRIVE
TEMPE, AZ 85266